PENGUIN BOOKS
THE VINTAGE SARDAR

Khushwant Singh was born in 1915 in Hadali, Punjab. He was educated at Government College, Lahore and at King's College and the Inner Temple in London. He practised at the Lahore High Court for several years before joining the Indian Ministry of External Affairs in 1947. He began a distinguished career as a journalist with All India Radio in 1951. Since then he has been founder-editor of *Yojna* (1951-1953), editor of the *Illustrated Weekly of India* (1979-1980), chief editor of *New Delhi* (1979-1980), and editor of the *Hindustan Times* (1980-1983). Today he is India's best-known columnist and journalist.

Khushwant Singh has also had an extremely successful career as a writer. Among the works he has published are a classic two-volume history of the Sikhs, several novels (the best known of which are *Delhi*, *Train to Pakistan* and *The Company of Women*), and a number of translated works and non-fiction books on Delhi, nature and current affairs. His autobiography, *Truth, Love and a Little Malice* was published in 2002.

Khushwant Singh was Member of Parliament from 1980-1986. Among other honours he was awarded the Padma Bhushan in 1974 by the President of India (he returned the decoration in 1984 in protest against the Union Government's siege of the Golden Temple, Amritsar).

GW00759007

THE VINTAGE SARDAR
The Very Best of
Khushwant Singh

PENGUIN BOOKS

PENGUIN BOOKS

Published by the Penguin Group

Penguin Books India Pvt. Ltd, 11 Community Centre, Panchsheel Park,
New Delhi 110 017, India
Penguin Group (USA) Inc., 375 Hudson Street, New York,
New York 10014, USA
Penguin Group (Canada), 90 Eglinton Avenue East, Suite 700, Toronto,
Ontario, M4P 2Y3, Canada (a division of Pearson Penguin Canada Inc.)
Penguin Books Ltd, 80 Strand, London WC2R 0RL, England
Penguin Ireland, 25 St Stephen's Green, Dublin 2, Ireland (a division of
Penguin Books Ltd)
Penguin Group (Australia), 250 Camberwell Road, Camberwell,
Victoria 3124, Australia (a division of Pearson Australia Group Pty Ltd)
Penguin Group (NZ), 67 Apollo Drive, Rosedale, Auckland 0632,
New Zealand (a division of Pearson New Zealand Ltd)
Penguin Group (South Africa) (Pty) Ltd, 24 Sturdee Avenue, Rosebank,
Johannesburg 2196, South Africa

Penguin Books Ltd, Registered Offices: 80 Strand, London WC2R 0RL, England

First published by Penguin Books India 2002
This revised edition published by Penguin Books India 2011

Copyright © Naina Dayal 2002, 2011

10 9 8 7 6 5 4 3 2 1

ISBN 9780143417569

Typeset in Sabon by Mantra Virtual Services
Printed at Yash Printographics, Noida

Contents

Acknowledgements

I would like to thank P.R. Krishna Narayanan of Cochin who sent me copies of most of the pieces included in this collection. It was his idea that these be put together and published under the title, *The Vintage Sardar*.

For granting permission to include articles that appeared in the columns 'With Malice Towards One And All . . .', Gossip Sweet and Sour' and '. . . This Above All', my thanks to *Hindustan Times* and ABP Limited.

The Writerly Life

Journalist bashing

'Journalists are like dogs,' writes Philip Howard of *The Times* (London): 'When one barks, the whole pack takes up the howl, and for a week or two the world seems full of nothing but sentencing for rape, say. Then the subject becomes boring and the pack moves on.'

Howard is by no means alone in abusing journalists; there are many people who have as low an opinion of pressmen as he. Most of all those who have been bitten by them as politicians are regularly. Howard is also partly correct in his observation that when one journalist takes up an issue ('barks'), others are quick to join him ('take up the howl'). I can cite innumerable recent instances when one journalist broke a story which others took up and made it appear that nothing in the world mattered more than their obsessions at the time. There was the case of the blinding of prisoners in Bihar jails (broken by M.J. Akbar of *Sunday* and *The Telegraph*); the matter of Abdul Rehman Antulay's so-called charitable trusts (broken by Arun Shourie in *The Indian Express*); the training of Khalistani terrorists and the peccadilloes of Orissa's chief minister, J.B. Patnaik (exposed by Pritish Nandy in *The Illustrated Weekly of India*); Pakistan's claim to have developed nuclear weapons (exploded by Kuldip Nayar); the investigative reporting of topics of national interest done by teams of *The Statesman*'s reporters. I could multiply such instances by the dozen, but have deliberately chosen the more spectacular ones because

they did in fact bring about a change in the thinking of
the entire country. Can similar claims be made by
practitioners of any other profession?

*

I take up cudgels on behalf of my fraternity because
journalist-bashing has become a favourite pastime of
our politicians who are themselves as crooked as a
dog's hind legs. For them, any stick is good enough to
beat a dog (journalist) with. But of all people, when
politicians accuse journalists of corruption, it is enough
to make a dog laugh. Every dog has his day; today it
is the day of the politician: he is the top dog. It will not
last very long and I hope he may soon find himself an
underdog. People are beginning to realize that if
politicians continue to make a mess of all our
institutions as they already have of the legislature, the
bureaucracy and the judiciary, the country will go to
the dogs. The one institution that can stand up to them
and engage in a dog fight unto death is the free press.
The people must see to it that no one puts us in the dog
house.

The Hindustan Times, 28 March 1987

■

A London-Glasgow diary: Authors, Poets etc.

I was included amongst the few Third World writers to be present on the 70th birthday of Edwin Morgan who is acknowledged as Scotland's leading poet and the darling of Glaswegian intellectuals. I had not heard of him. The seminar entitled 'Writing Together' began with Morgan's lecture and recitation of his poems. I was in the last row of the hall; I could not catch all of what he was saying both because of the distance and because of his strong Scottish accent. Evidently some things he said were witty, as some of the audience responded with laughter. At the end of his lecture there was thunderous applause.

I realized I was out of touch with modern trends. After the lecture I happily retired to a corner with my plate of cold salad and a glass of wine. I eyed the motley collection of literary celebrities from Asia to Africa.

*

'Writing Together'. No writer worth his or her salt writes 'together' (with someone else). It is the most solitary of all professions in the world. The first session, however, is on *The Writer and Language*. Shirley Lim is Malaysian of Chinese origin. She does not write in either Chinese or Malay but in English. Her incentives, the scenery, sounds and smells are Malaccan but her expression is English. Should she feel guilty? No, your mother tongue is what you are able to express yourself best in. She reads some of her poems. An animated discussion follows on the ethics of writing in a language other than your own. Shirley is a great head-wagger agreeing enthusiastically with every sentence said by everyone. Her talk is followed by a panel discussion. I am charmed by the Scottish dialect (Cromarty Island) used by the Sikh, Gurmit Mattu, and the Glaswegian used by a Pakistani girl. She mourns the fact that despite her best efforts she is unable to express herself in Urdu which her parents use at home. Nigerian and Ghanaian writers pitch in with the problems they face speaking Yoruba but writing in English. I have never felt the conflict or pangs of conscience about speaking Punjabi, enjoying reading Urdu poetry but expressing myself only in English. Every conquering race has imposed its language on the conquered. Aryans imposed Sanskrit on Dravidians and adivasis; Muslim conquerors Turki, Arabic and Persian; the British imposed English. Altogether they enriched other languages. A pure language is the poorest in health; a mongrel language is full of vigour. English being the most bastardized is the healthiest and richest of them all—with the largest and ever increasing vocabulary. I use it because I love it.

The Hindustan Times, 26 May 1990

Our Indo-Anglian mistress

I spent an uproarious weekend in Chandigarh. The rightful tenants of the Raj Bhavan, Siddhartha and Maya Ray, were in Delhi, leaving me to wallow in the luxury of their estate with its dozens of impeccably well-mannered flunkeys at my beck and call. My only obligation was to address a gathering organized by the Vivek High School on the usage of Indian English. My task was lightened by more than half by Michael Hamlyn of *The Times* (the spinster-aunt of the best in English journalism). Hamlyn is one of the protégés of *The Times*' greatest editor, Sir William Rees-Mogg, whose guidebook to good journalism is Fleet Street's Bible. 'No sentence should have more than 24 words,' it lays down. 'Well, OK, if you can't manage in 24, you may have 34. Full stop.' You must not overload your sentences with redundant adjectives. Avoid repeating words which mean the same thing, eg. rules and regulations, unless and until, selfish egotism (Gandhiji's favourite), dreaded terrorist, etc.

Hamlyn was too polite to say anything rude about Indian journalism but could not resist having a few digs at 'Cops nabbing miscreants' while ministers were 'air dashing' to Delhi and back. Narayanan, editor of *The Tribune*, gently reminded him that in Fowler's *Modern English Usage,* all instances of abusage were taken from *The Times*. I provided the comic interlude between Hamlyn's well-educated list of Indian-English in our newspapers and questions from the audience.

As editor of *The Hindustan Times*, I did my best to make my correspondents and reporters avoid clichés and Indianisms. It was a losing battle. Meetings continued to be 'packed to capacity', speakers heard 'in pin drop silence', the police were perpetually 'swinging into action', pot-bellied state ministers continued to 'rush to Delhi', boys kept getting into trouble for 'eve-teasing'. In any case, the editorial blue pencil could not extend to the wire services provided by the PTI and UNI. They filled up (as they do today) more than half the pages of the paper.

Then there were Indian howlers in advertisements which I was told were none of my business. Most national dailies earn more revenue from their matrimonial ads for brides and grooms than those for livestock or machinery. How was I to tell lusty young men looking for mates that the word 'homely' does not mean one who can keep a tidy home, cook wholesome food and not cast her eyes at strange men, but a plain-looking, ugly girl! And that an unmarried girl is not necessarily a virgin. Obituary columns caused me the same agony. North Indians were always going to their 'heavenly abode'; Gujaratis were 'passing away'; Maharashtrians 'breathed their last'; and south Indians made quicker exit: they simply 'expired'.

It is easy to mock the poor Babu for importing Hindi reverences into the English language—'Dear and Respected Pitaji, *Charansparsh*'—or ending with an interrogatory offer: 'any service?' How can he be blamed when his boss is often 'not in his seat' and if on tour, is 'out of station?' Then there are half-baked masters of the pompous pen. To wit: 'With bulging biceps and tremendous triceps, he was unparalleled on the parallel bars.'

The best practitioners of conscious Indianisms are Raja Rao and Mulk Raj Anand. Raja Rao has a point when, instead of slurping piping hot tea, he slurps 'hot, hot' tea; or likes his glass of water to be 'cold, cold'. After 'nine, nine, ten, ten' years he comes to India to replenish his depleted stock of Indianisms. When I deprecate the use of such language, Mulk 'shows eyes at me' and tells me to stop 'eating his head'. I don't take offence at anything he says because he is like my 'real brother' and I 'love him like anything'.

Nissim Ezekiel's *Goodbye Party for Miss Pushpa T.S.* is perhaps the best example of Gujarati-English. It is too long to reproduce here but a few lines from Keki Daruwala's *The Mistress* sums up his and my gratitude to the bastard language. 'No one believes me when I say my mistress is half-caste,' he begins and traces her genealogy. He capsules his debt to his beloved in the last verse:

No, she is not Anglo-Indian
The Demellos would bugger me if they got scent of this,
And half my body would turn into a bruise.
She is not Goan, not Syrian Christian,
She is Indian English,

The language that I use.

Sunday, 19 December 1987

Banning Rushdie

Now that the Government has announced that Salman
Rushdie's *The Satanic Verses* is to be banned in India,
I would like to clarify my role in the affair. As
Consultant Editor of Penguin India, I read the
manuscript six months ago. I had predicted that the
Government of India would succumb to the pressure
of Muslim opinion and ban the book; and felt that we
(Penguin India) should distance ourselves from the
project—we would lose a lot of money and even expose
ourselves to the wrath of an intolerant public. However,
let me reiterate, I am against any kind of censorship
on books, periodicals or newspapers on any ground
whatsoever—religious, political or pornographic. What
an adult chooses to read is entirely his or her own
business. The only exception I would make to this
fundamental freedom of access to published material
is the duty to protect minors from exposure to writing
which might impair their mental development. I will
still exercise my right to re-read Rushdie's book if I
can lay my hands on it.

I recall some of the books banned by our Government

in recent years. Aubrey Menen's *Rama Retold*, a satire
on the Ramayana; Stanley Wolpert's *Nine Hours to
Rama* on the murder of the Mahatma; Arthur Koestler's
Lotus and the Robot which mocked our pretensions of
religiosity and Gandhism; Agehanand Bharati's *The
Ochre Robe*, a narration of his own conversion to
Hinduism and practices of the Dasanami order of
Sadhus. Menen's book sold out. Koestler's and Bharati's
are now commonly available in paperback at many
bookstores. Penguin India intends to publish *Nine Hours
to Rama*. Government censorship agencies have short
memories. I would recommend all four books to
readers as they are extremely well written and
provocative.

About the literary merits of Rushdie's *The Satanic
Verses*, I am somewhat confused. It is a very confusing
book with just about everything thrown in. A plane
approaching England is hijacked by Khalistanis led
by a winsome, iron-souled lass called Tavleen. The
plane crashes but two men survive, Gibreel Ferishta
(closely resembling Amitabh Bachchan) who sets about
acquiring a heroic-angelic image, and Saladin
Chamcha whose feet turn into hooves and horns grow
out of his head. The reader concludes that the theme
of the novel is God versus Satan, the contest between
good and evil. The author then discovers that there is
always some good in evil and some evil in good. The
confusion becomes worse confounded with the
appearance of another Gibreel, the archangel. An
epileptic girl leads a caravan of pilgrims to Mecca. A

prophet called Mahound receives contradictory revelations from the Almighty. Other characters include a woman mountaineer who is inspired by an earlier conquest to get on top of the Everest on her own. It is almost impossible to disentangle the different strands of fantasy that go into the making of the novel. The outcome of the contest between God and Satan is blurred beyond recognition in a sandstorm of disjointed events.

Rushdie has been paid an enormous sum in advance royalty. Banning of the book in India will undoubtedly be followed by similar bans in Islamic countries. This will ensure him bumper sales of the book all over the world. However, I fear he may have to limit the enjoyment of his royalties to Europe and north America. It was somewhat naive of him to say that books did not cause riots. I presume he has not heard of the fate that befell Mahashe Rajpal, author of *Rangeela Rasul* and Swami Shraddhananda. Both were murdered. Two years ago, the offices of *The Deccan Herald* in Bangalore were attacked by a mob. They had published a pointless short story which had nevertheless offended some Muslims. Hindu, Muslim or Sikh, our margin of tolerance is very narrow.

The Hindustan Times, 22 October 1988

Honouring an editor

I was invited to preside over a function in honour of V.N. Narayanan, editor of *The Tribune* of Chandigarh. I was vaguely aware of the cultural organization headed by Sudarshan Gour based in Shimla which honours writers, actors and artists—there are so many such award-giving organizations besides the Rotarians, Lions and others that one loses count of them. The number of awardees is also countless. However, since this time it was the editor of northern India's oldest and most prestigious newspaper edited by a South Indian during the most turbulent period of Punjab's history, I thought it my duty to accept. It gave me an opportunity to spell out my personal views on the responsibilities of an editor today.

To start with, I think the editor of an ongoing daily newspaper has not much scope to impose his personality on the journal he presides over. Most of its contents are taken from wire services like the PTI and UNI, from foreign and states correspondents if it has any, and its correspondents in district towns. All this is put together by his chief of bureau. He is left largely to writing editorials and deciding what else will go on the edit page. It was my experience as editor that the edit page of any paper is the least read. An editor who wishes to attract attention has to occasionally step out of the edit to the first page and do the lead story under his own name—as M.J. Akbar of *The Telegraph* often does, or explode some nation-shattering news—as Arun

Shourie is periodically known to do.

Not all editors can take the liberty of writing stories for the front page. In many cases the proprietors reserve this right to air their own points of view—either personally or through a hired scribe. Editors of the traditional school of journalism to which Narayanan belongs stick to writing leaders for the edit page. He does this with commendable finesse—because he has to keep the interests of the Board of Trustees, the advertisers and his complex readership in mind—and courage, because it needs guts to write unpalatable truths in a society where people are prone to reply to criticism with Sten gun and pistol. To wit:

> *Haq achha; magar haq kay liye*
> *koee aur marey, to aur achha,*
> *Tum bhee koee Mansoor ho jo*
> *soolee charho?*
> (Truth is good; but if somebody else dies to uphold the truth, it is better.
> Are you some kind of Mansoor that you should mount the scaffold?)

That is why many editors prefer to keep quiet when their clear duty is to speak up against evil. They prefer to wax eloquent on issues on which most people are agreed—ever strong on the stronger side. Hazlitt wrote: 'They are dreadfully afraid there should be anything behind the editor's chair, greater than the editor's chair. That is a scandal to be prevented at all risk.'

A powerful editor, though he may enjoy considerable social status, is usually loathed by politicians and not much loved by his staff or his readers. Politicians loathing him is understandable because they are themselves a loathsome lot who hate being told the truth about themselves. Since he has to see that his correspondents and reporters do not sell him tinctured stories, he has to often question their integrity. That does not make him a lovable boss. He has also to contend with narrow-minded readers who are ever eager to take offence at the most trivial of issues. An intolerant public has become a real menace to editorial independence.

An editor has to plough a lonely furrow. If he does so conscientiously, all he gets is job satisfaction. That is his only true reward. G.K. Chesterton composed a prayer for journalists which might well be adopted as the Hippocratic oath for all pressmen:

From all the new fear teaches,
From lies of tongue or pen,
From all the easy speeches,
From sale and profanation
Of their most precious word
Deliver us, O Lord.

Sunday, 4 November 1989

■

The Famous and
the Infamous

Maker of Modern India

Tributes paid by the Indian Press to Raja Rammohun Roy added very little to our existent textbook information summed up in the cliché, 'Maker of Modern India'. I was lucky to learn a little more about him from Justice Das, M.R.A. Baig and Air Chief Marshal Lal. It was the airman who drew attention to many facets of the Raja's life. Did you realize he lived closer to the time of Emperor Aurangzeb than to ours? And while his contemporaries, the Peshwas and Maharajah Ranjit Singh, were still fighting with matchlock, musket and sabre, Rammohun was addressing memoranda in impeccable prose on subjects like the freedom of the press, the right of Indians to sit on Grand Juries, the need to abolish passports, property rights for Hindu women, etc? Did you know he could read and write eleven languages: Sanskrit, Bengali, Hindi, Urdu, Persian (he edited a journal in Farsi), Arabic, Hebrew, Syriac, Greek, English, French? And wrote 38 books? That though he started learning English at the age of 24, in five years he was able to handle it well enough to merit praise from Jeremy Bentham, who said that the Raja's letters were the work of an 'Englishman of superior education'.

Surely this man must have had the touch of genius! I can't think of any Indian, living or dead, who could match his achievements. This is all the more remarkable because Rammohun Roy had an indifferent education and an unhappy life. He was in constant argument with his father (his favourite word in dialogue was *kintu*—but), his mother took him to court, his wives (he was married to three women while he was a child) lived away from him, the fanatic Dharma Sabha made many attempts to have him killed.

None of this shook Rammohun Roy's faith in his mission. In the Brahmo Samaj he formulated a religion for the thinking Indian shorn of idolatry, ritual and belief in the supernatural. So reminiscent of poet Browning's statement: 'There is a new tribunal now, higher than God's, the educated man's.' The Raja's letter to Prince Talleyrand set out his faith in more precise terms: 'Not religion only but unbiased common sense as well as accurate scientific research leads us to the conclusion that all mankind is one great family of which numerous nations and tribes are only various branches.' This is exactly what Tom Paine said later: 'The world is my country, mankind my brethren, to do good, my religion.

Rammohun, despite his iconoclasm and flirtations with Islam and Christianity, never wavered in his loyalty to Hinduism. When he went to England he took his brahmin cooks with him (also two Indian cows). The last words he spoke before sinking into a coma were: *Hari Om*. He was buried with his sacred thread on him.

On every aspect of life—political, social, economic religious, literary or cultural—he left the impact of his personality. What made Mahatma Gandhi call him a 'pigmy'? It would be apparent to any student of history that Rammohun Roy was one of the greatest sons of India. Poet Tagore's riposte to Gandhiji was right; he described the Raja as 'a great-hearted man of gigantic intelligence'.

The Illustrated Weekly, 11 June 1972

■

Raj Thapar

There was a time when if asked to name a single couple who I could honestly say had found fulfilment in marriage, I would begin my enumeration with the names of Romesh and Raj Thapar. Now I don't know who to begin with because on the morning of the 10th April, Raj succumbed to cancer.

Marriage is a rotten, man-made institution. It survives because we have not been able to devise any better man-woman relationship that would provide security for our offspring. Marriage corrodes the personalities of both husband and wife, and most couples put up with it as best as they can by becoming indifferent, frequently unfaithful, bored and irritated with each other. Few have the energy or the courage to face social censure and call it off. Rarely, if ever, does a monogamous union turn out to be an exhilarating and a jointly creative venture of a lifetime. It did in the case of the Thapars.

They first met in Gulmarg when he was 16 and she 14. It blossomed into a Romeo-Juliet kind of romance which was consummated five years later following a

civil marriage. Neither of them had any use for
religious ritual. They never quarrelled; got on better
with each other than with anyone else and became
living examples of the Indian ideal, *ek jyoti doey moorti*
(one light in two bodies). They set up home in Bombay.
For some years Romesh edited *Crossroads* for the
Communist Party of India while Raj wrote books for
children in Hindi and English which were illustrated
by her English friend Rachel Grenfell. Two of them,
Seventh Daughter of the Sun and *Introducing India*,
sold out. Romesh soured of his association with the
CPI, closed down *Crossroads* and tried his hand at
films. He acted with Dilip Kumar and Meena Kumari
in *Footpath* before deciding that he was not cut out to
be a film star. In 1958 he launched the journal *Seminar*
with his wife as co-editor. Three years later, they shifted
to Delhi to be able to look after Romesh's ailing father.

The Thapars became the most sought after couple
in New Delhi's social circles. Wherever they went,
controversy was sure to follow. He was as forthright
in his speech as he was clear headed. She was always
beside him sparkling with wit and humour. Debate
was always animated, never acrimonious. They
became Mrs Gandhi's confidantes. Many men and
women who became ministers or ambassadors owed
their rise to the Thapars' recommendations. I do not
know when or why they fell out with the prime minister
and her family. It was Romesh who, with his
characteristic acerbic tongue, described Rajiv Gandhi's
ménage of advisers as a *Babalog* government.

Two years ago Raj developed symptoms of cancer. She was flown out to London for surgery. The doctor asked her if she had had a traumatic experience in the recent past which could have brought on the dreaded disease. She had. It was the massacre of Sikhs following Mrs Gandhi's assassination. The Thapars had given shelter to many Sikh families in their home and helped others to be moved to places of safety. She had put up a brave face but something inside her had snapped. She knew she had not very long to live.

A month before her death, Raj Thapar wrote her will. There was to be no announcement of the event in the newspapers. For her funeral, she chose a red cotton sari to symbolize the *Suhaag* (matrimonial bliss) in which she was going. There was to be no religious ceremony, nor *Chautha*. While her body lay on the floor under a heap of flowers, taped music of the Dagar brothers singing *Dhrupad* filled the room along with the incense. At the electric crematorium, there was *keertan* by her favourite *raggis* but no *ardas*.

Amongst the things that Raj has left behind is an unfinished manuscript of her autobiography, *All These Years*. She was worried that she may not be able to finish it and asked of God for no more than three months' grace to her to write the last chapter: 'Let not the thread of my song be cut while I sing, and let not my work end before its fulfilment' (Rig Veda).

The prayer was not answered.

I am told the autobiography has lethal stuff about people in power then and now. I hope Romesh will write the last chapter for her and honour her dying wish that 'not a line is to be deleted or changed'. On the 26th of April, Raj Thapar would have celebrated her 60th birthday.

The Hindustan Times, 25 April 1987

■

Shri 420

The one thought that kept cropping up in my mind from the day Raj Kapoor was taken ill while receiving the Dadasaheb Phalke award till after his death in Delhi and funeral in Bombay was how unfortunate it would be to die at the same time as a celebrity of his calibre. With the nation preoccupied with mourning the passing of a superstar, there would be few tears left to be shed on anyone else's demise.

There has been so much of Raj Kapoor in all the media by people close to him and better qualified to pronounce on him as a person and an actor, that anything I say may sound audacious. I saw no more than three of his films and met him only once. By then he had given up acting and taken to directing films. I had passing acquaintance with his father, Prithviraj Kapoor, for whom I had vast admiration. I had also enjoyed the hospitality of the Shashi-Jennifer home. Other members of the distinguished family I had only seen at a distance at airports or in airbuses. The one close encounter I had with Raj was sometime in the mid-1970s when he was busy producing *Satyam Shivam Sundaram*. The invitation came through Devyani Chaubal. I extended it to members of the Sindhi family who lived in a flat above mine. They were very excited about it. Sheila, a young attractive widow, dressed herself in a bright red sari; her daughter, Jyoti, in a blue sequined one, and their 12-year-old maid-servant, Fatima, in her best *salwar kameez*. The only other guest was Zeenat Aman who was playing the main role in the film. I introduced them to my guests. Raj took one long approving look at Sheila and decided that there was more to my friendship with her than met the eye. He promptly dubbed her *Laal Pari*.

We took our seats in his little cinema attached to his home-cum-studio. He sat alone in the front row, the rest of us behind him. I had Zeenat on my right, *Laal Pari*, her family and Devyani on the other. He explained what he had in mind in making the film. I was surprised at his excellent command of English and the way he articulated his thoughts. Who when asked, 'Do actors need brains?' answered, 'If they can act, no. If they can't, yes.' Raj Kapoor obviously had both brains and acting talent. At the time, only ten minutes of the shooting had been completed. Lights were dimmed. Scotch and a variety of kababs, fish fingers and chicken *tikkas* were passed around. I saw the opening shots: Zeenat emerging out of a lotus pool, filling her pitcher, knotting up her hair and slowly coming up the stairs, her wet flimsy sari clinging to her sinuous body and exposing her shapely bust. Raj turned round and said with great enthusiasm, 'Isn't she beautiful? I am a bosom man. What is a woman without bosom! You tell me?'

'All men are bosom men,' I replied. 'But you think this will pass the censor?'

'. . . the censor. He'll probably see it a dozen times before saying no. I'll put it back after he's okayed the rest of it.'

How can one ever forget anyone like him? Warm-hearted as only people of the old North-West Frontier are, unassuming as one who could mock himself to give others a laugh, gifted beyond measure, connoisseur of all that was beautiful; a crystal clear character with no *val chchal*—deviousness. There was nothing fraudulent about this '420'.

■

Akbar's love life

Emperor Akbar had 5000 women of all nationalities and religions in his harem. Of these, some 300 were Spanish or Portuguese. They introduced Akbar to wines from their country. Instead of his usual once-in-three-months visit, he sought their company more frequently. His favourite European was a Portuguese blonde he named *Dilruba* (heart warmer) who was an expert belly dancer. Till his forties the Emperor took a virgin to his *Khwaabgah* (dream chamber) every full-moon night.

No woman save the Hindu, Jodha Bai, was invited to the dream chamber more than once.

Akbar also enjoyed the Timurid privilege of asking his nobles to divorce their wives if he fancied them. At one time he had no less than a thousand divorcees at his disposal. They were treated as second class members of the royal seraglio, given less pocket money and poorer gifts. The one exception was Sakina, wife of Shaikh Obaidullah of Lahore, whom he acquired in 1564. She was a woman of extraordinary beauty and charm, described by those who saw her as 'a miracle of God's craftsmanship'. The poor Shaikh languished away, and died pining for Sakina. On his death, Akbar put an end to the royal prerogative of taking other men's wives. His son, Jehangir, respected his father's wish. When he fell in love with Sher Afghan's wife, Mehrunnissa (Noor Jahan) he did not ask him to divorce her. He had him murdered.

The Hindustan Times, 11 June 1988

■

Zia-ul-Haq

They called him *Surmay vaali Sarkar*—the ruler with *kohl* in his eyes. He had dark rims round his deep-set eyes; two teeth protruding like those of Brer Rabbit beneath his whiskers. He was not much to look at: short, stocky, nondescript.

They made lots of jokes about him—that even Allah

would not trust him and let him occupy his throne for a moment lest he refuse to get up. They said he was misusing Pakistan by doing to it what he should have been doing only to his Begum.

They did not love him. They did not hate him. They feared him a little, respected him a lot. Unlike other rulers of Third World countries, there was never a breath of suspicion about his making money, having extra-marital affairs, favouring relations or friends, being vindictive to those who crossed his path. He was a clean man and as square as square could be. He was upright and God-fearing.

He was remarkably free of the high self-esteem and arrogance that come with power. He was the most courteous of men, an observer of old-world etiquette: a thorough gentleman; the best public relations officer for himself and his country.

He was a man of myopic vision who saw everything through Islamic spectacles. This made him a hero of Muslim fundamentalists but anathema to the forward-looking who hoped to give their women equal rights, freedom from the veil and take the Muslim world from medieval backwardness towards commercial and industrial prosperity.

Although a soldier, Zia knew more about politics than most politicians. He kept his own counsel, confided in no one and never let army officers, bureaucrats or senior politicians get too big for their shoes and dream of replacing him. He was not devious but could outsmart all of them. He also had an uncanny sense of timing and knew when to strike. He was quicker than his adversaries in drawing his gun and shooting them down. They realized that the only way they could achieve their ambitions was to get him unawares and kill him. That is precisely what they did.

It would be stretching praise too far to say that with the death of Zia-ul-Haq, India has lost a friend. He befriended India's enemies. He extended hospitality to the likes of Ganga Singh Dhillon and Jagjit Singh Chauhan. He connived at giving encouragement, arms and shelter to Khalistani terrorists. He had no love for them, but by keeping our Punjab in a state of turmoil, he ensured the safety of his country's eastern frontier. He was more than a match for our leaders and often succeeded in making them look ham-handed and foolish. He was a formidable adversary.

I am sorry to see him go. With him in power, we at least knew where we stood in our relations with our great neighbour. Now it will be guesswork, astrology and gazing into crystal balls.

The Hindustan Times, 27 August 1988

■

The Edwina-Nehru affair

I was the press officer at the Indian High Commission when Panditji came to attend the first Commonwealth

Prime Ministers' Conference. For months before his visit, I had occupied a room on the first floor of India House; the copper plate beside the door bore the legend 'Countess Mountbatten of Burma'. My high commisioner, Krishna Menon, who knew which side his bread was buttered, went out of his way to kowtow to people who mattered to Prime Minister Nehru. The Mountbattens were on top of this list. Menon hoped Lady Mountbatten would become a regular visitor to India House. I was under instructions to clear out of the room within five minutes' notice leaving no trace of my having used it. Her Ladyship never entered the room reserved for her. His Lordship did once by force of circumstances: by mistake, he turned up half an hour early for a reception.

I was one of the India House staff ordered to be present at Heathrow Airport when Prime Minister Nehru arrived. It was a cold winter night. We were lined up to be introduced to him. 'What are you fellows doing here at this time of the night?' he asked us. 'Go home and get some sleep.' He was pleased to see us, his minions, assembled to salaam him. At Krishna Menon's insistence, I went to Panditji and asked, 'Sir, will you be needing my service? I am your PRO.' He snapped back, 'What, at this hour? Go home!'

The next morning, the front page of the *Daily Herald* carried a large picture showing a lady in her negligee opening the door to let in Prime Minister Nehru. The caption read: 'Lady Mountbatten's midnight visitor.' It went on to add that Lord Mountbatten was not in

London. The press photographer had taken a chance to get this scoop. After getting to know the way Krishna Menon's mind worked, I would not put it beyond him to have tipped off the editor. When I came to India House, he told me that the prime minister was furious with me and I had better keep out of his way for a few days. So I did.

A day before the prime minister was due to return home, he invited Edwina Mountbatten to dine with him at a Greek restaurant in Soho. When the two were seated at a corner table, a battery of press photographers arrived on the scene. Next morning, many London papers carried pictures taken in the cosy basement of the Greek cafe. This time there was no escape. I was summoned to Claridges Hotel. As I entered Panditji's bedroom, he looked me up and down to ask me who I was. I had been with him for an entire week. 'Sir, I am your press officer,' I replied. 'You have strange notions of publicity,' he said in a withering tone. At the time, it did not occur to him or to me that the only person who could have tipped off the press was Krishna Menon. Menon had a mind like a corkscrew.

However, there seems to be no doubt that there existed some kind of emotional, and possibly even physical attachment between the Lady and the prime minister. Examine the profiles of the two: You will be startled by the resemblance. There is usually a strong element of narcissism in the choice of one's beloved. But Edwina was by no means the only woman in Panditji's life even while this affair was on. Catherine

Clement (author of *Edwina and Nehru: A Novel*), who started her research shortly before Rajiv Gandhi was assassinated, had to wade through more than 11,000 photographs and hundreds of letters to write her book. When asked what she thought of this relationship, she replied, 'Beautiful! It was simply beautiful!'

The Hindustan Times, 20 April 1996

■

Phoolan Devi

It was the afternoon of Saturday, 14 February 1981. Winter had given way to spring. Amidst the undulating sea of ripening wheat and green lentil were patches of bright yellow mustard in flower. Skylarks rose from the ground, suspended themselves in the blue skies and poured down song on the earth below. Allah was in His heaven and all was peace and tranquillity in Behmai.

Behmai is a tiny hamlet along the river Jamuna inhabited by about fifty families belonging mainly to the Thakur caste, with a sprinkling of shepherds and ironsmiths. Although it is only eighty miles from the industrial metropolis, Kanpur, it has no road connecting it to any town. To get to Behmai you have to traverse dusty footpaths meandering through cultivated fields, and go down narrow, snake-infested ravines choked with camelthorn and elephant grass. It is not surprising

that till the middle of February, few people had heard
of Behmai. After what happened on Saturday the 14th,
it was on everyone's lips.

There was not much to do in the fields except drive
off wild pigs and deer. Some boys armed with catapults
and loud voices were out doing this; others played on
the sand bank while their buffaloes wallowed in the
mud. Men dozed on their charpoys; women sat in
huddles gossiping as they ground corn or picked lice
out of their children's hair.

No one in Behmai noticed a party dressed in police
uniforms cross the river. It was led by a young woman
with cropped hair wearing the khaki coat of a deputy
superintendent of police with three silver stars, blue
jeans and boots with zippers. She wore lipstick and
her nails had varnish on them. Her belt was charged
with bullets and had a curved Gurkha knife—a *kokri*—
attached to it. A Sten gun was slung across her
shoulders and she carried a battery-fitted megaphone
in her hand. The party sat down beside the village
shrine adorned with the trident emblem of Shiva, the
God of destruction.

The eldest of the party, a notorious gangster named
Baba Mustaqeem, instructed the group on how to go
about their job: A dozen men were to surround the
village so that no one could get out; the remaining
men, led by the woman, were to search all the houses
and take whatever they liked. But no women were to
be raped nor anyone except the two men they were
looking for, to be slain. They listened in silence and

nodded their heads in agreement. They touched the base of Shiva's trident for good luck and dispersed.

The girl in the officer's uniform went up on the parapet of the village well, switched on the megaphone and shouted at the top of her voice, 'Listen you fellows! You *bhosreekey* (progenies of the cunt)! If you love your lives, hand over all the cash, silver and gold you have. And listen again! I know those *madarchods* (motherfuckers) Lal Ram Singh and Shri Ram Singh are hiding in this village. If you don't hand them over to me I will stick my gun into your bums and tear them apart. You've heard me. This is Phoolan Devi speaking. If you don't get cracking, you know what Phoolan Devi will do to you. *Jai* Durga *Mata* (Victory to the Mother Goddess, Durga)!' She raised her gun and fired a single shot in the air to convince them that she meant what she said.

Phoolan Devi stayed at the well while her men went looting the Thakurs' homes. Women were stripped of their earrings, nose pins, silver bangles and anklets. Men handed over whatever cash they had on their persons. The operation lasted almost an hour. But there was no trace of Lal Ram Singh or Shri Ram Singh. The people of the village denied ever having seen them. 'You are lying!' roared Phoolan Devi. 'I will teach you to tell the truth.' She ordered all the young men to be brought before her. About thirty were dragged out to face her. She asked them again, 'You motherfuckers, unless you tell me where those two sons of pigs are, I will roast you alive.' The men pleaded with her and swore they had never seen the two men.

'Take these fellows along,' she ordered her men. 'I'll teach them a lesson they will never forget.' The gang pushed the thirty villagers out of Behmai along the path leading to the river. At an embankment, she ordered them to be halted and lined up. 'For the last time, will you tell me where those two bastards are, or do I have to kill you?' she asked pointing her Sten gun at them. The villagers again pleaded ignorance. 'If we knew, we would tell you.' 'Turn round,' thundered Phoolan Devi. The men turned their faces towards the green embankment. '*Bhosreekey*, this will also teach you not to report to the police. Shoot the bloody bastards!' she ordered her men and yelled, '*Jai* Durga *Mata*!' There was a burst of gunfire. The thirty men crumpled to the earth. Twenty died; the others hit in their limbs or buttocks lay sprawled in blood-spattered dust.

Phoolan Devi and her murderous gang went down the path yelling, '*Jai* Durga *Mata*! *Jai* Baba Mustaqeem! *Jai* Bikram Singh! *Jai* Phoolan Devi!'

The next morning, the massacre of Behmai made front-page headlines in all newspapers all over India.

*

Dacoity in India is as old as history. In some regions it is endemic and no sooner are some gangs liquidated than others come up. The most notorious dacoit country is a couple of hundred miles south-west of Behmai,

along the ravines of the Chambal river in Madhya
Pradesh. In the Bundelkhand district of Uttar Pradesh
in which Behmai is located, it is of comparatively recent
origin and the State police suspect that when things
became too hot around the Chambal, some gangs
migrated to Bundelkhand where the terrain was very
much like the one they were familiar with. The river
Jamuna, after its descent from the Himalayas, runs a
sluggish, serpentine course past Delhi and Agra into
Bundelkhand. Here it passes through a range of low-
lying hills covered with dense forests. Several monsoon-
fed rivulets running through deep gorges join it as it
goes on to meet the holy Ganga at Allahabad. It is
wild and beautiful country: hills, ravines and forests
enclosing small picturesque hamlets. By day there are
peacocks and multicoloured butterflies; by night,
nightjars calling to each other across the pitch-black
wilderness flecked by fireflies. Nilgai, spotted deer,
wild boar, hyena, jackal and fox abound. It is also
infested with snakes, the commonest being cobras, the
most venomous of the species. Cultivation is sparse
and entirely dependent on rain. The chief produce are
lentils and wheat. The peasantry is amongst the poorest
in the country. The two main communities living along
the river banks are Mallahs (boatmen) and Thakurs.
The Thakurs are the higher caste and own most of the
land. The Mallahs are amongst the lowest in the Hindu
caste hierarchy, own little land and live mostly by
plying boats, fishing and distilling liquor. Till recently,
dacoit gangs were mixed: Thakurs, Mallahs, Yadavs

(cattlemen), Gujjars (milkmen) and Muslims. But now, more and more are tending to becoming caste-oriented. There is little love lost between the Thakurs and the Mallahs. Behmai is a Thakur village; Phoolan Devi, a Mallahin.

No stigma is attached to being a dacoit; in their own territory they are known as *bagis* or rebels. Hindi movies, notably the box office hit of all time, *Sholay*, in which the hero is a dacoit, has added romance to the profession of banditry.

Dacoit gangs are well-equipped with automatic weapons, including self-loading rifles acquired mostly through raids. A police note on anti-dacoity operations records that Jalaun district which includes Behmai, has fifteen gangs of between ten to thirty members each operating in the area. Phoolan Devi and her current paramour, Man Singh Yadav, have fifteen men with them. In the last six months, the police have had ninety-three encounters with dacoits in which they killed 159 and captured 137. Forty-seven surrendered themselves. 439 still roam about the jungles and ravines, hunting and being hunted.

I sat on the parapet of the village well, on the same spot from where Phoolan Devi had announced her arrival in Behmai a year and a half earlier. In front of me sat village men, women and children and the police escort provided for me. An old woman wailed, 'That Mallahin killed my husband and two sons. May she die a dog's death!' A man stood up and bared his belly which showed gun-shot scars. Another bared his buttocks and pointed to a dimple where a bullet had hit him.

'Can any of you tell me why Phoolan Devi came to this village and killed so many people?' I asked.

No one answered.

'Is it true that Lal Ram Singh and Shri Ram Singh were in Behmai?'

A chorus of voices answered: 'No, we have never seen them.'

'Is it true that a few months before the dacoity they had brought Phoolan Devi with them, raped her for several weeks before she managed to escape?'

'*Ram! Ram!*' protested some of them. 'We had never seen the Mallahin in this village before the dacoity.'

'Why then, did she ask for the two brothers? How did she know her way about this village?'

No one answered.

'You will not get anything out of these fellows,' the police inspector said to me in English. 'You know what these villagers are! They never tell the truth.'

I gave up my cross-examination and decided to go around Behmai. I started from the village shrine with the Shiva's trident, came back to the well and then to the embankment where she had killed the twenty men. I went up a mound where the police had set up a sentry box from which I could get a bird's-eye view of the village, the Jamuna and the country beyond. The police sentinel on duty who had been in the village for several weeks volunteered the following information: 'Sir, I think I can tell you why Phoolan Devi did what she did. You see that village across the Jamuna on top of the hill? It is called Pal, it is a Mallah village. Mallahs used to come through Behmai to take the ferry. Thakur boys used to tease their girls and beat up their men. I am told there were several instances when they stripped the girls naked and forced them to dance. The Mallahs appealed to Phoolan Devi to teach these Thakurs a lesson. She had her own reasons as well. Her lover Bikram Singh had been murdered by Thakurs Lal Ram Singh and his twin brother Shri Ram Singh. And they had kept her imprisoned in this village for several weeks, raping and beating her. She managed to escape and rejoin her gang. She also suspected that these fellows have been informing the police of her movements. It was revenge, pure and simple.'

*

'For every man this girl has killed, she has slept with two,' said the superintendent of police in charge of 'Operation Phoolan Devi'. The police estimate the number of men slain by her or one of her gang in the last year and a half to be over thirty. There is no way of finding out the exact number of men she murdered or was laid by. But it is certain that not all the killings nor the copulations were entirely of her own choosing. On many occasions she happened to be with bandits who were trigger-happy; and being the only woman in a gang of a dozen or more, she was regarded by them as their common property. She accepted the rules of the game and had to give herself to them in turn. It was more a resignation to being raped than the craving for sex of a nymphomaniac.

I was able to reconstruct Phoolan Devi's past by talking to her parents, sisters and one of her lovers, and cross-checking what they told me with a statement she made to the police on 6 January 1979, the first time she was arrested. This was in connection with a robbery in the house of her cousin with whom her father had had a dispute over land. Some stolen goods were recovered from her. She spent a fortnight in police custody. Her statement is prefaced by a noting made by the officer. He describes her as 'about twenty years old; wheatish complexion, oval face; short but sturdily built.' Phoolan Devi stated: 'I am the second daughter of a family of six consisting of five girls. The youngest is a boy, Shiv Narain Singh. We belong to the Mallah caste and live in the village Gurh-Ka-Purwa. At the age of twelve I was given away in marriage to a forty-five-year-old widower, Putti Lal.' Then she talks of her second 'marriage' to Kailash in Kanpur. The rest of her life story was narrated to me by her mother, Muli. 'Phoolan Devi was too young to consummate her marriage and came back to us after a few days. A year or two later, we sent her back to her husband. This time she stayed with him for a few months but was unhappy. She came away without her husband's permission, determined not to go back to him.' It would appear that she had been deflowered. Her mother describes her as being 'filled up'—an Indian expression for a girl whose bosom and behind indicate that she has had sex. It would appear that she had developed an appetite for sex which her ageing husband could not fulfil. Her parents were distraught: a girl leaving her husband brought disgrace to the family. 'I told her to drop dead,' said her mother. 'I told her to jump in a well or drown herself in the Jamuna; we would not have a married daughter living with us. Putti Lal came and took away the silver ornaments he had given her and married another woman. What were we to do? We started looking for another husband for her, but it is not easy to find a husband for a discarded girl, is it?' she asked me. Phoolan Devi kept out of her parents' way as much as she could by taking the family's buffaloes out for grazing. She began to liaise with the son of the village headman. (In rural India such affairs are consummated in lentil or sugarcane fields.) The headman's son invited his friends to partake of the feast. Phoolan Devi had no choice but to give in. The village gossip mill ground out stories of Phoolan Devi being available to anyone who wanted to lay her. Her mother admitted, 'The family's *pojeeshun* (position) was compromised; our noses were cut. We decided to send her away to her sister, Ramkali, who lives in Teonga village across the river.'

It did not take long for Phoolan Devi to find another lover in Teonga. This was a distant cousin, Kailash, married and with four children. Kailash had contacts with a dacoit gang. He gives a vivid account of how he was seduced by Phoolan Devi. 'One day I was washing my clothes on the banks of the Jamuna. This girl brought her sister's buffaloes to wallow in the shallows of the river. We got talking. She asked me to lend her my cake of soap so that she could bathe herself. I gave her what remained of the soap. She stripped herself before my eyes. While she splashed water on herself and soaped her bosom and buttocks, she kept talking to me. I got very excited watching her. After she was dressed, I followed her into the lentil fields. I threw her on the ground and mounted her. I was too worked up and was finished in no time. I begged her to meet me again. She agreed to come the next day at the same time and at the same place.

'We made love many times. But it was never enough. She started playing hard to get. "If you want me, you must marry me. Then I'll give you all you want," she said. I told her I had a wife and children and could only have her as my mistress. She would not let me touch her unless I agreed to marry her. I became desperate. I took her with me to Kanpur. A lawyer took fifty rupees from me, wrote something on a piece of paper and told us that we were man and wife. We spent two days in Kanpur. During the day we went to the movies; at night we made love and slept in each other's arms. When we returned to Teonga, my parents refused to take us in. We spent a night out in the fields. The next day I told Phoolan Devi to go back to her parents as I had decided to return to my wife and children. She swore she would kill me. I have not seen her since. But I am afraid one of these days she will get me.'

'What does your Phoolania look like?' I asked Kailash. 'I am told her sister Ramkali resembles her.'

'Phoolan is slightly shorter, lighter-skinned and has a nicer figure. She is much better-looking than Ramkali.'

'I am told she uses very bad language.'

'She never spoke harshly to me; to me she spoke only the language of love.'

Phoolan Devi had more coming to her. A few days after she had been turned out by Kailash, she ran into Kailash's wife Shanti, at a village fair. Shanti pounced on Phoolan, tore her hair, clawed her face and in front of the crowd that had collected, abused her: 'Whore! Bitch! Homebreaker!' What was known only to a few hamlets now became common knowledge: Phoolan was a slut. As if this were not enough, the village headman's son who was under the impression that Phoolan was exclusively at his beck and call, heard of her escapade with Kailash. He summoned her to his house and thrashed her with his shoes. Thus, at the age of eighteen, Phoolan found herself discarded by everyone. Her parents did not want her, her old husband had divorced her, her second 'marriage' had come to naught, she had been laid by men none of whom was willing to take her as a wife. It seemed to her that no one in the world wanted to have anything to do with her. She had only two choices before her: to go to some distant city and become a prostitute, or kill herself. There were times she considered throwing herself into the well.

Unknown to her, there was someone who had taken a fancy to her. This was young Bikram Singh, a friend of Kailash and member of a gang of dacoits led by a man called Babu Gujjar. Bikram Singh had seen Phoolan around the village and heard stories of her performances in the lentil fields. One afternoon he came to Gurh-Ka-Purwa with some of his gang and bluntly told Phoolan's parents that he had come to take away their daughter. Phoolan was adamant. 'I will talk to you with my sandals,' she said, spitting on the ground. Bikram hit her with a whip he was carrying. Phoolan Devi fled from the village and went to stay with her other sister, Rukmini, in the village Orai. It was there that she heard that a warrant for arrest had been issued against her and Kailash for the dacoity in her cousin's house. The man who took her to the police station raped her before handing her over. She spent a fortnight in jail. When she returned home, Bikram came to see her again. He threatened her: 'Either you come with me or I take your brother Shiv Narain with me.' Phoolan was very attached to her only brother; he was eleven years old and studying in the village school. After some wrangling, she agreed to go with Bikram.

Kailash describes Bikram Singh as fair, tall and wiry. Bikram was obviously very taken with Phoolan. He had her long hair cropped. He gave her a transistor radio and cassette recorder as she was inordinately fond of listening to film music. He bought her a khaki shirt and jeans. He taught her how to handle a gun. She proved a very adept disciple and was soon a crack shot.

For the first time in her life Phoolan felt wanted by someone. She responded to Bikram's affection and began to describe herself as his beloved. She had a rubber stamp made for herself which she used as a letterhead in the letters she got written on her behalf. It reads: '*Dasyu Sundari, Dasyu Samrat* Bikram Singh *ki Premika*' (Dacoit Beauty, Beloved of Bikram Singh King of Dacoits).

Being the 'beloved of Bikram' did not confer any special privileges on Phoolan. Whether she liked it or not, she had to serve the rest of the gang. At the time, the leader happened to be Babu Gujjar, a singularly rough customer. He had his own way of expressing his superiority over his gang. He liked to have sex in broad daylight and in front of the others. So Phoolan Devi had to submit to being ravished and brutalized by Babu Gujjar in public. When her turn came to be made love to by Bikram, she complained to him about the indignity. By then, Bikram had developed a strong sense of possession over Phoolan. He did not have the courage to admit it, but one night while Babu Gujjar was asleep, he shot him in the head. Bikram Singh became the leader of the gang and at Phoolan's insistence, forbade the others from touching her. There wasn't much resentment because the gang soon acquired another woman, Kusum Nain, who happened to be better-looking than Phoolan. Kusum, a Thakur, attached herself to the Thakur brothers, Lal Ram Singh and Shri Ram Singh. The two women became jealous of each other.

Despite her many unpleasant experiences with men, Phoolan Devi did not give up her habit of cock-teasing. She sensed that her full bosom and rounded buttocks set men's minds aflame with lust. Nevertheless, she persisted in bathing in the presence of the men of her gang. One gangster, now in police custody, who had known her as well as Kusum Nain and Meera Thakur (other female dacoits, since then slain) vouches for this: 'The other girls were as tough as Phoolan but they observed certain proprieties in the company of men. They would go behind a tree or bushes to take a bath. Not Phoolan; she took off her clothes in front of us as if we did not exist. The other girls used language becoming to women. Phoolan is the most foul-mouthed wench I have ever met. Every time she opens her mouth she uses the foulest of abuse—*bhosreekey, gaandu* (bugger), *madarchod, betichod* (daughterfucker).'

The inspector of police has in his files a sheaf of letters written to him on behalf of Phoolan Devi. They are a delightful mixture of the sacred and the profane, of highfalutin Hindi and sheer obscenity. The one he read out to me began with salutations to the Mother Goddess under her printed letterhead. The text ran somewhat as follows:

Honourable and Respected Inspector General Sahib,
I learn from several Hindi journals that you have been making speeches saying that you will have us dacoits shot like pie-dogs. I hereby give you

notice that if you do not stop *bakwas* (nonsense) of this kind, I will have your revered mother abducted and so thoroughly fucked by my men that she will need medical attention. So take heed.

It is more than likely that Bikram Singh, besides keeping Phoolan Devi exclusively for himself, also claimed his right as the leader to enjoy the company of Kusum Nain as well. This irked the Thakur brothers. They left Bikram's gang and looked out for an opportunity to kill him. On the night of 13 August 1980, they trapped and slew Bikram Singh. It is believed that the murder was committed in Behmai, and that the Thakurs unceremoniously kicked Bikram's corpse before it was thrown into the river.

Lal Ram Singh and Shri Ram Singh retained Phoolan Devi in Behmai. They brutalized and humiliated her in front of the entire village. One night, on the pretext of wanting to relieve herself, Phoolan Devi managed to vanish into the darkness. She crossed the Jamuna over to the Mallah village, Pal. From there she got in touch with the Muslim gangster Baba Mustaqeem and pleaded with him to help her avenge the murder of Bikram Singh. Mustaqeem agreed. This is how she ended up being at Behmai on the afternoon of 14 February 1981.

■

Amrita Shergil

I am hardly justified in describing Amrita Shergil as a woman in my life. I met her only twice. But these two meetings remain imprinted in my memory. Her fame as an artist, her glamour as a woman of great beauty which she gave credence to in some of her self-portraits, and her reputation for promiscuity snowballed into a veritable avalanche which hasn't ended to this day and gives me an excuse to include her in my list.

One summer, her last, I heard that she and her Hungarian cousin-husband who was a doctor had taken an apartment across the road where I lived in Lahore. He meant to set up a medical practice; she, her painting studio. Why they chose to make their home in Lahore, I have no idea. She had a large number of friends and admirers in the city. She also had rich, landowning relatives on her Sikh father's side who regularly visited Lahore. It seemed as good a place for them to start their lives as any in India.

It was June 1941. My wife had taken our seven-month-old son, Rahul, for the summer to my parents' house, 'Sunderban', in Mashobra, eleven miles beyond Shimla. I spent my mornings at the High Court gossiping with lawyers over cups of coffee or listening to cases being argued before judges. I had hardly any case to handle myself. Nevertheless, I made it a point to wear my black coat, white tabs around the collar and carry my black gown with me to give others an appearance of being very busy. I returned home for lunch and a long siesta before I went to play tennis at the Cosmopolitan Club.

One afternoon I came home to find my flat full of the fragrance of expensive French perfume. On the table in my sitting room-cum-library was a silver tankard of chilled beer. I tiptoed to the kitchen, asked my cook about the visitor. 'A memsahib in a sari,' he informed me. He had told her I would be back any moment for lunch. She had helped herself to a bottle of beer from the fridge and was in the bathroom freshening up. I had little doubt my uninvited visitor was none other than Amrita Shergil.

For several weeks before her arrival in Lahore I had heard stories of her exploits during her previous visits to the city before she had married her cousin. She usually stayed in Faletti's Hotel. She was said to have made appointments with her lovers with two-hour intervals—at times six to seven a day—before she retired for the night. If this was true (men's gossip is less reliable than women's) love formed very little part of Amrita's life. Sex was what mattered to her. She was a genuine case of nymphomania, and according to her nephew Vivan Sundaram's published account, she was also a lesbian. Her modus vivendi is vividly described by Badruddin Tyabji in his memoirs. One winter when he was staying in Shimla, he invited Amrita to dinner. He had a fire lit for protection from cold and Europian classical music playing on his gramophone. He wasted the first evening talking of literature and music. He invited her again. He had the same log fire and the same music. Before he knew what was happening, Amrita simply took her clothes off and lay stark naked on the carpet. She did not believe in wasting time. Even the very proper Badruddin Tyabji got the message.

Years later, Malcolm Muggeridge, the celebrated author, told me that he had spent a week in Amrita's parents' home in Summer Hill, Shimla. He was then in the prime of his youth—his early twenties. In a week she had reduced him to a rag. 'I could not cope with her,' he admitted. 'I was glad to get back to Calcutta.'

A woman with the kind of reputation Amrita enjoyed drew men towards her like iron filings to a magnet. I was no exception. As she entered the room, I stood up to greet her. 'You must be Amrita Shergil,' I said. She nodded. Without apologizing for helping herself to my beer she proceeded to tell me why she had come to see me. They were mundane matters which robbed our first meeting of all romance. She wanted to know about plumbers, dhobis, carpenters, cooks, bearers etc. in the neighbourhood whom she could hire. While she talked I had a good look at her. Short, sallow-complexioned, black hair severely parted in the middle, thick sensual lips covered in bright red lipstick, stubby nose with blackheads visible. She was passably good looking but by no means a beauty.

Her self-portraits were exercises in narcissism. She probably had as nice a figure as she portrayed herself in her nudes but I had no means of knowing what she concealed beneath her sari. What I can't forget is her brashness. After she had finished talking, she looked around the room. I pointed to a few paintings and said, 'These are by my wife; she is an amateur.' She glanced at them and scoffed, 'That is obvious.' I was taken aback by her disdain but did not know how to retort. More was to come.

A few weeks later I joined my family in Mashobra. Amrita was staying with the Chaman Lals who had rented a house above my father's. I invited them for lunch. The three of them—Chaman, his wife Helen and Amrita, came at midday. The lunch table and chairs were lined on a platform under the shade of a holly oak which overlooked the hillside and a vast valley. My seven-month-old son was in the playpen teaching himself how to stand up on his feet. He was a lovely child with curly brown locks and large questioning eyes. Everyone took turns to talk to him and complimented my wife for having produced such a beautiful boy. Amrita remained lost in the depths of her beer mug. When everyone had finished, she gave the child a long look and remarked, 'What an ugly little boy!' Everyone froze. Some protested at the unkind remark. But Amrita was back to drinking her beer. After our guests had departed, my wife said to me very firmly, 'I am not having that bloody bitch in my house again.'

Amrita's bad behaviour became the talk of Shimla's social circle. So did my wife's comment on her. Amrita got to know what my wife had said and told people, 'I will teach that bloody woman a lesson she won't forget;

I will seduce her husband.'

I eagerly awaited the day of seduction. It never came. We were back in Lahore in the autumn. So were Amrita and her husband. One night her cousin Gurcharan Singh (Channi) who owned a large orange orchard near Gujranwala turned up and asked if he could spend the night with us, as Amrita, who had asked him over for the weekend, was too ill to have him stay with her. The next day, other friends of Amrita's dropped in. They told us that Amrita was in a coma and her parents were coming down from Summer Hill to be with her. She was an avid bridge player and in her semi-conscious moments mumbled bridge calls. The next morning I heard that Amrita was dead.

I hurried to her apartment. Her father, Sardar Umrao Singh Shergil, stood by the door in a daze, mumbling a prayer. Her Hungarian mother went in and out of the room where her daughter lay dead, unable to comprehend what had happened. That afternoon, no more than a dozen men and women followed Amrita's cortège to the cremation ground. Her husband lit her funeral pyre. When we returned to her apartment, the police were waiting for her husband. Britain had declared war on Hungary as an ally of its enemy, Nazi Germany. Amrita's husband was therefore considered an enemy because of his nationality, and had to be detained in prison.

He was lucky to be in police custody. A few days later, his mother-in-law, Amrita's mother, started a

campaign against him accusing him of murdering her
daughter. She sent letters to everyone she knew asking
for a full investigation into the circumstances of her
daughter's sudden death. I was one of those she sent a
letter to. Murder it certainly was not; negligence,
perhaps. I got details from Dr Raghubir Singh who
was our family doctor and the last person to see Amrita
alive. He told me that he had been summoned at
midnight. Amrita had peritonitis caused perhaps by a
clumsy abortion. She had bled profusely. Her husband
asked Dr Raghubir Singh to give her blood transfusion.
The doctor refused to do so without fully examining
his patient. While the two doctors were arguing with
each other, Amrita quietly slipped out of life. But her
fame liveth evermore.

■

The one and only Nirad Babu

'There is nothing more dreadful to an author than
neglect, compared with which reproach, hatred and
opposition are names of happiness.' These words of
Dr Johnson were inscribed by Nirad Chaudhuri on my
copy of his book, *A Passage to England*. These words
hold the key to Nirad's past life and present personality.
They explain the years of neglect of one who must
have at all times been a most remarkable man; his
attempt to attract attention by cocking-the-snook at

people who had neglected him; and the 'reproach, hatred and opposition' that he succeeded in arousing as a result of his rudeness.

Nirad had been writing in Bengali for many years. But it was not until the publication of his first book in English, *The Autobiography of an Unknown Indian*, that he really aroused the interest of the class to which he belonged and which, because of the years of indifference to him, he had come heartily to loathe— the Anglicized upper-middle class of India. He did this with calculated contempt. He knew that the wogs were more English than Indian, but were fond of proclaiming their patriotism at the expense of the British. That having lost their own traditions and not having fully imbibed those of England, they were a breed with pretensions to intellectualism that seldom went beyond reading the blurbs and reviews of books.

He therefore decided to dedicate the work 'To the British Empire . . .' The wogs took the bait, and having only read the dedication, sent up a howl of protest. Many people who would not have otherwise read the autobiography, discovered to their surprise that there was nothing anti-Indian in its pages. On the contrary, it was the most beautiful picture of eastern Bengal that anyone had ever painted. And at long last, India had produced a writer who did not cash in on naïve Indianisms but could write the English language as it should be written—and as few, if any, living Englishmen could write.

Nobody could afford to ignore Nirad Chaudhuri any

more. He and his wife Amiya became the most sought-after couple in Delhi's upper-class circles. Anecdotes of his vast fund of knowledge were favourite topics at dinner parties.

The first story I heard of the Chaudhuri family was of a cocktail party hosted by the late Director-General of All India Radio, Colonel Lakshmanan. Nirad had brought his wife and sons (in shorts and full boots) to the function. After the introductions, the host asked what Nirad would like to drink, and mentioned that he had some excellent sherry.

'What kind of sherry?' asked the chief guest. Colonel Lakshmanan had, like most people, heard of only two kinds. 'Both kinds,' he replied. 'Do you like dry or sweet?' This wasn't good enough for Nirad, so he asked one of his sons to taste it and tell him. The thirteen-year-old lad took a sip, rolled it about his tongue, and after a thoughtful pause replied, 'Must be an Oloroso 1947.'

Nirad Babu could talk about any subject under the sun. There was not a bird, tree, butterfly or insect whose name he did not know in Latin, Sanskrit, Hindi and Bengali. Long before he left for London, he not only knew where the important monuments and museums were, but also the location of many famous restaurants. I heard him contradict a lady who had lived six years in Rome about the name of a street leading off from the coliseum—and prove his contention. I've heard him discuss stars with astronomers, recite lines from obscure fifteenth century French literature and advise a wine dealer on the best vintages from Burgundy. At a small function in honour of Laxness, the Icelandic winner of the Nobel Prize for literature, I heard Nirad lecture him on Icelandic literature.

Nirad was a small, frail man, little over five feet. He led a double life. At home he dressed in *dhoti-kurta* and sat on the floor to do his reading and writing. When leaving for work, he wore European dress: coat, tie, trousers and a monstrous khaki sola topi. As soon as he stepped out, street urchins would chant 'Johnnie Walker, left, right, left, right.'

Nirad Babu was not a modest man; he had great reason to be immodest. No Indian, living or dead, wrote the English language as well as he did. He was also a very angry man. When he was dismissed from service by a singularly half-baked I&B minister, Dr B.V. Keskar, he exploded with wrath. Years later, the Government of India wanted him to do a definitive booklet on the plight of the Hindu minority in East Pakistan and offered him a blank cheque for his services. Nirad, who was in dire financial straits, turned it down with contempt. 'The Government may have lifted its ban on Nirad Chaudhuri, but Nirad Chaudhuri has not lifted his ban on the Government of India,' he said to me when I conveyed Finance Minister T.T. Krishnamachari's proposal to him.

Chaudhuri's second book, *A Passage to England*, received the most glorious reviews in the English press. Three editions were rapidly sold out and it had the distinction of becoming the first book by an Indian author to have become a bestseller in England. The bay windows of London's famous bookshop, Foyle's, were decorated with large-sized photographs of Nirad. Some Indian critics were, as in the past, extremely hostile. Nirad's reaction followed the same pattern. At first he tried not to be bothered by people 'who didn't know better', then burst with invective against the 'yapping curs'. I asked him how he reconciled himself to these two attitudes. After a pause he replied, 'When people say nasty things about my books without really understanding what I have written, I feel like a father who sees a drunkard make an obscene pass at his daughter. I want to chastise him.' Then, with a typically Bengali gesture demonstrating the form of chastisement, 'I want to give them a shoe-beating with my *chappal*.'

A few years ago Nirad Babu wrote an article for a prestigious London weekly in which he mentioned how hard he was finding life in Oxford, living on his royalties from books. I published extracts from it in my column. K.K. Birla wrote to me to tell Nirad Babu that he would be happy to give him a stipend for life for any amount in any currency he wanted. I forwarded Birla's letter to Nirad. He wrote back asking me to thank Birla for his generous offer, but refused to accept it. It is a pity that he accepted a CBE (Commander of the British Empire) from the British Government. He deserved a peerage, because he was in fact, a peerless man of intellect and letters.

The Hindustan Times, 14 August 1999

Death and the
Afterlife

Old age and retirement

A sizeable part of my mail consists of letters from gentlemen who describe themselves as senior citizens and pensioners. Their general tenor is that nothing is being done in the country for old people who are unable to fend for themselves. Most of them are from men in their late 60s and 70s; a few from octogenarians. I write back expressing my lack of sympathy. I am as old as most of them, if not older. In my 70s I am working harder than I did in my 40s. And earning a lot more than I ever have. No wasting time in prayers, temple-going, looking after grandchildren or taking my walking stick for an airing in the park. I can understand that really old people (I would put the minimum qualifying age at 80), who have no one to look after them, or are sick or senile, should be provided accommodation in old people's homes. But others have no business to be doing nothing but watching TV or boring their friends with stories of their past days— that is unpardonable anecdotage. This kind of defeatism is best left to poets:

*Na poochh kaun hain, kyon raah
mein laachaar baithey hain
Musafir hain, safar karney kee
tamanna haar baithey hain.*
(Don't ask me who I am, why I sit
helplessly by the roadside;
I am a traveller who has lost the

will to go to my destination.)

Don't hark back to the days of your youth. You will never be able to recapture them or do what you did in younger days. That can be self-defeating and frustrating.

> *Javaanee jaatee rahee, aur hamen*
> *pataa na chalaa*
> *Isee ko dhoond rahey hain, kamar*
> *jhukaye hooey.*
> (Youth has vanished, and I never
> got to know about it
> I keep looking for it with my back
> doubled with age.)

In my third year as editor of *The Hindustan Times*, when my contract was due for renewal, my *anndaataa*, K.K. Birla, asked me, '*Sardar Sahib, aap ke retire honey kaa vichaar naheen*—aren't you thinking of retiring?' I was then 69. I replied, '*Birlaji, retire to main Nigambodh Ghaat mein hoonga* (I will retire when I am taken to the cremation ground).' Actually, I plan to be buried so that my rotten guts can enrich the soil of my motherland after I have gone.

The Hindustan Times, 1 July 1989

■

Life after death

Dr Satya Vrat Shastri, professor of Sanskrit of Delhi University, returned from a lecture tour of Europe and North America to hear the announcement of an award of Rs 25,000 from the Sanskrit Akademi of Uttar Pradesh. Felicitations!

Amongst the many topics he lectured on was the concept of death in the Upanishads. He tells me that in Italy his audience included doctors of medicine and scientists. They were impressed by what he had to say. I can well understand it because to intelligent Westerners brought upon Hebraic, Christian and Islamic beliefs, the Hindu-Jain-Buddhist-Sikh concept of Samsara—birth, death and rebirth—appears altogether more sophisticated than their theories of the Day of Judgement, heaven and hell.

The question remains unanswered: Is there any rational basis for believing that there is life after death? Our scriptures (Hindu, Jain, Buddhist and Sikh) state categorically that there is. Most of this belief is taken from the Upanishads and summarized in the Gita. It is maintained that on death, the body dies but the soul lives on. The soul changes bodies as a person changes his or her clothes. The Kathopanishad asserts that birth, decay and death occur only to the material body but there is something beyond the body which does not perish. It is the *atman* hidden in the heart's cavity. 'Every seventh year all the particles of the body change and get renewed but still one is the same person; the

identity never changes.' The question is, what is the
foundation of this identity? Shastriji answers: 'It means
the unchangeable something within beings which is
the source of intelligence and existence and upon which
our relative existence depends. The *atman* or the
permanent entity is birthless . . . and deathless.'

What exactly *atman* is remains shrouded in mystery
answered by the negative, not this, not that. It is all-
pervasive *parmatma* as well as individual *jivatman*.
When the latter merges into the former, *jyoti jyot
milay*—your light mingles with eternal light (Adi
grantha), and a person achieves liberation (*moksha*)
from the cycle of birth, death and rebirth.

At the same time, our Hindu theology also provides
a system of reward and punishment through the theory
of transmigration of souls as well as an interregnum,
the state of limbo in which the soul subsists awaiting
decision whether to be reborn as a good person for
good deeds or as vermin as punishment for evil acts in
previous life.

'By argument one cannot explain what exists after
death; *naisa tarkana matir apaneya*,' concedes Dr
Shastri. 'There cannot be any scientific proof that the
atman exists after death, it is ever present in the sense
that it cannot be verified.' So why labour with
argument: those who believe will go on believing, those
who don't are not likely to be converted by jugglery of
beautiful phrases. As far as I am concerned, death
remains the final full stop. I am, however, more than
eager to unravel its mystery and join believers in the

prayer:

> *Asato ma sad gamaya*
> *Tamaso ma jyotir gamaya*
> *Mrtyor ma amrtam gamaya.*
> (Lead me from unreality to reality
> Lead me from darkness to light
> Lead me from death to immortality.)
> *The Hindustan Times, 18 June 1988*

Experience of death

There is sizeable literature of the experiences of people who were declared medically dead, i.e. their hearts had stopped beating but were revived within a few minutes. Most talk of being able to hear their relations crying over them, dazzling lights and soft music. Sceptics dismiss these experiences as pre-conditioned hangovers common to people believing in God, heaven, hell and the afterlife. None of these beliefs applies to Professor A.J. Ayer who was declared dead but whose heart began to beat again after four minutes. He has published his 'postmortem' experiences in a series of articles.

First let me introduce you to Ayer who did me the privilege of dining in my home about 30 years ago. Sir Alfred Julius Ayer (born 1910) was educated at Eton and Christ Church College, Oxford. He became a professor of logic and taught at various prestigious universities including his alma mater. He made his name in 1936 with the publication of *Language, Truth & Logic* as an exponent of logical positivism. His other works include *The Foundations of Empirical Knowledge* (1940) and *The Problem of Knowledge* (1956). Ayer is recognized as England's foremost free thinker and agnostic.

When he 'died' two months ago and came back to life four minutes later, he recorded his experience in an article entitled 'That Undiscovered Country'. He admitted that 'my recent experiences have slightly weakened my conviction that my genuine death will be the end of me'. In a later article he somewhat qualified his belief in the full-stop theory of death saying 'my experiences have weakened, not my belief that there is no life after death, but my inflexible attitude towards that belief'.

Did Ayer really die and get to 'the other side'? Doctors attending on him hold that although his heart had stopped beating, his brain continued to function. But they added that as soon as the heart stops beating, the brain functioning goes into rapid decline and comes to a halt within four minutes. Ayer's post-mortem experiences were, at best, recollections of an impaired brain.

Ayer summarily dismisses the Judeo-Christian-Muslim belief in the resurrection of the body. None of them tell us in what form the dead will be resurrected—

as they were when they died or as young people in good health? What about the young who die in infancy, cripples, and those born mentally defective? Will we be reborn in the same sex? Will we carry memories of our present lives into our future lives?

Ayer is equally dismissive of the re-incarnation theory to which Hindus, Jains, Buddhists and Sikhs subscribe. However, he concedes that if there comes a time when people can really recall experiences of prior lives in greater abundance than hitherto provided, there may be cases for 'licensing reincarnation'. So far it is no better than science fiction.

The Hindustan Times, 29 October 1988

■

Learning from the dead

Cemeteries have long been my favourite places of recreation. I wouldn't be seen dead in one at night because I have this mortal dread of ghosts. But on a bright, sunny day, I'd rather take a stroll through a cemetery than through any well- laid park or garden. For one, there are not many people living who share my enthusiasm; for another, seeing the hundreds that I have outlasted lying at my feet gives me a sense of having triumphed over them. I read their epitaphs and murmur to myself, 'O poor sod! Born after me; gone before me.' And then I go on to read the next tombstone.

In Washington I was lucky to have an apartment close to Arlington cemetery, the largest in the country spreading over hundreds of acres—a green hillside dipping into the Potomac river. Every Sunday morning, hail, rain or snow, I found myself striding along furlong after furlong of tombstones. Since Arlington is primarily meant to house remains of those who fell in battle and their wives, most graves bear only names, dates of birth and demise of their tenants. Only old graves have epitaphs eulogizing the worldly greatness of their occupants. Quite a few presidents of the United States are buried in Arlington. I was surprised to learn how many had come to a violent end. Of these, the most celebrated was John F. Kennedy, whose grave on the top of the hill is Arlington's chief attraction. Bus-loads of tourists come from all parts of the world to have themselves photographed by the flame which burns round the clock and read the many inspiring messages he delivered which are inscribed in a stone round a small amphitheatre. Besides the Kennedy mystique that makes this a hallowed spot, it is the panoramic view it commands that attracts crowds. You get an uninterrupted view of the Potomac from the northern to the southern horizon, and across the river, the Kennedy Centre and the Lincoln and Washington memorials right upto Capitol Hill. On a clear day it is a grand spectacle.

Americans, though they are big on flag waving (Stars and Stripes banners are displayed on most big buildings), do not indulge in hero-worship as much as we do. On the contrary, exploring the seamier, sexier sides of political leaders, captains of industry and celebrities is a national pastime. On the many mornings I was at Kennedy's grave, I rarely met an American, whereas Russians, Chinese, Japanese and Indians came by the bus-load.

The crest of Arlington cemetery is older and its graves more ornate with the usual paraphernalia of angels, quotes from the Bible and eulogies for the dead. Also, many graves are mounted with equestrian statues. My friend Orekhov of the Soviet embassy, pointed them out to me and asked, 'Do you know that when a horse has one of its legs raised, it means that he fell in the field of battle?' 'The horse or the rider?' I asked. 'Not the horse; the man riding it. It is a well-established statutory convention observed in Europe and North America.'

I bet you didn't know that. We do not observe this convention. Most of our Shivaji statues have his horse with one fore-leg raised. He did not die in battle. Those justified in having them would be warriors like Tipu Sultan and Rani Lakshmibai of Jhansi.

Sunday, 14 May 1988

The Question of Faith

Not in the name of Allah

Driving along Janpath the other day, I ran into a mammoth assemblage of Muslims at prayer on the lawns of the Boat Club. It was a spectacular sight—as congregational prayers of Muslims always are—with hundreds of thousands of men in serried ranks, bowing, kneeling and standing up with military precision. I recalled Allama Iqbal's moving description:

> *Aa gayaa ain laraaee mei agar vat-e-namaaz*
> *Qibla roo ho kay zameen bose hooee Qaum-e-Hijaaz*
> *Ek hee saf mein kharey ho gayey Mahmood-o-Ayaaz*
> *Na koee banda rahaa aur na koee banda-nawaaz.*
> (In the midst of raging battle if time came to pray,
> Hejazis turned to Mecca, kissed the earth and ceased from fray.
> Sultan and slave in single file stood side by side.
> Then no servant was, nor master, nothing did them divide.)

Then come two memorable lines:

> *Banda-o-Sahab-o Muhtaaj-o-Ghanee ek hooey*
> *Teyree Sarkar mein pahuncahay to sabhee ek hooey*
> (Between serf and lord, needy and rich, difference there was none

73

When they appeared in Your court, they came as
equals and one.)

What followed this impressive demonstration of
Ittehaad (unity) of the *millat* (community) was far from
elevating. No sooner had the prayer ended with the
gesture of turning right and left invoking *Salaam* (peace)
on mankind, than came torrents of words which were
far from peaceful. The Imam Sahib of Jama Masjid
spoke of burning down Ministers' houses, breaking
people's legs, smashing their motor cars. I fled from
the scene. I had acquired a new Maruti only the day
before.

My mind continued to be troubled for many hours.
For some months I have begun my mornings reading
five *suras* of the Quran. That day I had finished reading
Moti Lal Jatwani's *Sufis of Sindh*. The Imam's words
of hate had nothing in common with the teaching of
the holy book nor the songs of love of Sufi saints, all
of whom were devout Muslims. Jotwani's short thesis
(he deals with five Sufis, notably, Shah Abdul Latif of
Bhit) cleared the dilemma in my mind. There have
always been two kinds of Muslims: the bigots and the
benign. Bigots preached intolerance and persecuted
Sufis who stood for accommodation with non-Muslims.
Mansur Al Hallaj and Sarmad were two among
hundreds who earned martyrdom because they refused
to toe the line of bigotry. What made Islam acceptable
to millions of Indians was the Islam of Sufis like Farid
Shakarganj, Moinuddin Chisti, Nizam-ud-din Aulia

and Hazrat Mian Mir. Men who created prejudice against Muslims were desecrators of temples, idol-breakers and those who preached hatred and violence. It is time the Muslims told the Imam Sahib what disservice he did to Islam.

The Hindustan Times, 11 April 1987

■

The power of silence

There is more to silence than keeping one's mouth shut. You have to shut out external noises as well as the tumult within you to realize what immense power it can generate. Our ancients from the times of the Jain Tirthankars and Gautam the Buddha down to Mahatma Gandhi and Vinoba Bhave observed periods of silence. Those who could, retreated to mountains or forests to get away from the clamour of cities; those who could not, shut themselves in their rooms and meditated.

I have yet to learn how to meditate and still the tumult in my mind. But I am fortunate enough to be able to spend long hours (sometimes days) by myself. I can vouch for the difference not speaking and not listening to anyone makes. There are days when I have to attend conferences, cocktail parties and receptions, meet lots of people and listen to a lot of small talk. By the evening, I feel done in. The days I spend in my study reading and writing with the telephone off the hook, I do not feel tired. By the evening, I am rejuvenated.

Our culture has become highly verbalized. 'To understand' has come to mean 'to be able to communicate'. It is impossible to communicate without opening your mouth. When a philosopher once asked the Buddha, 'Without words, without the wordless, will you tell me the Truth?'

The Buddha replied by keeping silent.

The word 'silence' is derived from the Greek *hesuchia*. John Climacus (late 16th century) in his book *The Ladder of Divine Ascent* writes, '. . . the beginning of *hesuchia* is to throw off all noise as disturbing for the depth of the soul. And the end of it is not to fear disturbances and to remain insusceptible to them.' Surely, earplugs could successfully cut off external noises! What Climacus must have meant by becoming insusceptible to them was to cultivate stillness of the mind. Much earlier, Plutarch had observed, 'We learn speech from men; silence from the gods.' You can avoid speech, but true silence has to be cultivated. The Sufi Abu Yazid al-Bistani (9th century) once said: 'No lamp I saw brighter than silence; no speech I heard better than speechlessness.'

These savants were concerned with the mystic value of silence. Not being a mystic, I can only commend the virtues of silence in worldly affairs. Besides recharging one's inner batteries, it has many other uses. It can be the decisive winner in an angry dialogue. Chesterton called it 'the unbearable repartee'; Bernard

Shaw described it as 'the most perfect expression of scorn'. As still waters run deep so does a man of silence conceal what he has within him. It is truly said: 'Beware of a man who does not talk and of a dog that does not bark.'

The Hindustan Times, 7 March 1987

■

Human face of God

I asked for an audience with the Dalai Lama. I did not intend to question him about the Chinese occupation of his homeland—which to me is as immoral as the Russian occupation of Afghanistan now fortunately coming to an end. Rulers of China are not bothered about political morality nor yield to pressures of world opinion. So there was no point in my making the Dalai Lama talk of the offer of compromise settlement he had made recently, and its outright rejection by the Chinese. I was more intrigued by his claim that Buddhism is a more sophisticated religion than others as it strongly stresses rationality and is very modern in its sensitivity. He had gone on to say, 'for those types who want to follow a path of sceptical inquiry and reason rather than a path of faith, Buddhism may prove useful.' The Buddha himself said, 'Do not believe in anything merely because I said it. Be like an analyst buying gold, cutting and burning the substance to test it in every way. Accept it only when it meets the full criteria of reason, and when it proves to be of benefit to you.' That kind of attitude is compatible with modern scientific outlook.

I arrived in Dharamsala where the Dalai Lama has been in residence since his exile from Tibet. The upper part of the mountain range known as McLeod Ganj has become a little Tibet in India: Tibetan schools, libraries, a medical institute, a separate township for 1,500 children, temples, and over 50 restaurants serving Tibetan food. You hear more Tibetan spoken there than the local Pahari dialect of Kangra.

Before I tell you of my question and answer session, let me tell you about the Dalai Lama's background. He was one of 16 children of a peasant family of eastern Tibet, of which only seven survived their infancy. At the age of two he was picked up by the national committee charged with the duty of finding the incarnation of the 13th Dalai Lama who had died in 1933. Two years later, he was brought to Lhasa and proclaimed His Holiness Tenzin Gyatso, the 14th Dalai Lama. However odd this system of locating successors may sound to sceptical ears, it has an enormous advantage over other political or social systems: from childhood, a boy is trained to take over the responsibilities of a spiritual and secular leader of his people. He does not have to be the eldest son of a King to become the Prince of Wales nor the son of a President or a prime minister to be the heir presumptive. By the time he takes over his responsibilities, he is fully acquainted with his job. Tibetan Buddhism does not separate politics from religion. The 14th Dalai Lama is Tibet's secular and spiritual monarch.

I waited my turn to be received. A group of monks came out with a boy of five with his head shaved. He had been discovered as a re-incarnation of another Lama and initiated by His Holiness. A German couple waiting before us in the queue was ushered in. Fifteen minutes later we were asked to go in. The Dalai Lama stood outside his reception room—a tall, powerfully built man wreathed in smiles of welcome. We presented the traditional silk scarfs, shook hands and were escorted to our seats.

'Your Holiness, I am not going to ask you about politics. My questions will be on matters of religion. I am an agnostic and they may sound impertinent. I ask to be forgiven before I begin.'

He laughed uproariously and took my hand. 'In that case I can relax. I have to be very careful about politics: you may ask what you like.'

I had my list of questions ready: How did life originate? Is there a God? If so, why is there so much injustice and wickedness in the world? Are there rewards and punishments for good or evil deeds done in life? What is death—the destruction of body and mind or only the body? Is there a life hereafter or a rebirth after death?

The Hindustan Times, 16 July 1988

∎

Why the fast of Ramazan?

I had vague notions of why Muslims fast during Ramazan. So I asked my Muslim friends and read up all I could find in my library. I write this for the benefit of my non-Muslim readers in the conviction that knowledge of beliefs of our fellow citizens creates better understanding.

Of all the months of the Muslim calendar, Ramazan or Ramadan is the only one designated as felicitous—*shareef* in India, *mubarak* in Arabic. The observance of fast during this month is next to *namaaz* (prayer), the second most important pillar of Islam—the other two being *zakat* (charity) and *Haj* (pilgrimage). The month is divided into three ten-day periods (*ashra*). The first is devoted to *rehmat* (kindness), the second to *mafrat* (forgiveness) and the third to insurance against being consigned to hell. The most important, *Leilatul* (Night of Wonder), falls in the last ten days of the lunar month and is usually observed on the 27th. According to a *Hadith*, while the reward for other good works is given by angels, the reward for fasting is given by Allah himself.

Apart from the good that occasional fasting does to the body, the real purpose of the Ramadan fast is to give people personal experience of what hunger and thirst are like so that they can better appreciate the pangs the poor suffer from deprivation. It cleanses the body of accumulated poison and cleanses the soul of unconcern for the suffering of the underprivileged.

Contrary to popular belief, the fast does not begin with sunrise but well before it, when the eastern horizon begins to turn grey. This Ramazan, it was around 4 a.m. Strict watch is kept on the time, as eating or drinking even a minute after the prescribed time can invalidate the fast. It ends with the setting of the sun when it is broken with *Iftari*—a light repast of dates or fruit. Throwing large receptions to gain political leverage is exploitation of a solemn religious rite.

Of the three *Eids* (days of rejoicing), the *Eid-ul-Zuha* or *Bakr-id* (Eid of sacrifice), *Eid-e-Millaad-un-Nabi* (the Prophet's birthday) and the one following the end of Ramadan on the first day of the next month, *Shawwel,* this is the most auspicious and is known as *Eid-ul-Fitr.*

The tradition of fasting is pre-Muslim, and was practised by the Jews as well as the Pagans. In Arabia it was known as *tahannuth*, the month of asceticism. People observed it by fasting from sunrise to sunset, abstaining from other wordly pleasures and meditating on their doings. The Prophet himself spent this month in a cave in Mount Hera, a short distance from Mecca, taking his wife Khadija and servants with him. It was during this month that one night (known as the Night of Wonder, *Leilatul Qadr*), he heard the voice of God commanding him to read (Iqrra). The Prophet, being illiterate, was unable to do so. The order was repeated three times before the Prophet recited the very first revelation which, in the course of years, became the Quran.

Proclaim!
In the name of thy Lord and cherisher who created,
Created man out a mere clot of congealed blood.
Proclaim!
And thy Lord is most bountiful
He who taught the use of the pen
Taught man that which he knew not . . .

There is another reference in the Quran to the Night of Wonder:

We have indeed revealed this message
In the Night of Power
And what will explain
To thee what night of power is?
The night of power
Is better than a thousand months
Therein came down
The angels and the Spirit
By God's permission
On every errand
Peace!
This until the rise of morn.

It is believed that it was after this revelation that the Prophet asked his followers to face Mecca instead of Jerusalem when they prayed, and fixed Friday as the day for special congregational prayers. It was also in the month of Ramadan many years later that the Prophet returned from Medina to Mecca as its liberator.

He was questioned by two followers on the merits of abstention. 'It is not *riza* or self-torture,' he replied, 'it fortifies the body and the soul till they become a shield. It will protect you from evil till holes are made in it.'

'And what makes these holes?' asked his companions.

'Falsehood and calumny,' replied the Prophet.

For the Shias, Ramadan has added significance as it was during this month that Hazrat Ali received an injury to which he succumbed three days later. They spend three days in mourning.

After Eid prayers, a collection (*fitra*) is made to be disbursed amongst the poor and the needy.

I exhort my non-Muslim friends to join me in wishing our Muslim brethren *Eid-Mubarak*.

The Hindustan Times, 14 May 1988

■

God incarnate

It is not often that one meets a person worshipped by thousands as a reincarnation of Sri Rama and Sri Krishna, the long awaited Kalki Avatar with power to raise the dead and manifest himself to his disciples thousands of miles away from him. I do not believe in *avatars* or miracles. But I am fascinated by people whose lives have been changed by contact with such phenomena. This is how it happened:

'I am Kapahi of the World Prayer Movement,' said the voice on the phone.

'I do not believe prayers can save the world from disaster,' I replied cutting him short. 'I am an agnostic.'

'I know,' he persisted, 'Guruji also knows you are an agnostic. But he wants to meet you.'

The appointment was made. Kapahi came to pick me up. We drove past Aurobindo Ashram into a side road and pulled up in front of a modest-sized unpretentious bungalow. Kapahi took off his shoes; I slipped off my sandals. He ran the palms of his hands on the floor of the verandah and smeared the dust on his forehead: for him the bungalow was the temple of God. A young man rushed forward, shook me by the hand and said, 'He's waiting for you.'

In the room cluttered with books and pictures, was a bed. Reclining against the pillow was a frail man in his 80s with a saffron bandana tied round his head. He was busy writing Urdu poetry. He put down his pen and stretched both his arms towards me. Before I could touch his feet (I am a compulsive feet-toucher), he took me in his embrace. I broke down. It seemed to me as if this was my tryst with destiny.

This was Bhola Nath Ji. The young man who had conducted me to the room was his younger son, Priya Nath Mehta. He had given up his career as a nuclear physicist at Harvard to look after his father. His brother practises medicine in England.

'I have waited a long time for you,' began Bhola Nath Ji and quoted a Persian couplet about *visal*—the meeting of lovers. He took my hand in his and went on talking non-stop for almost an hour. His repertoire of Sanskrit, Persian, Urdu and Punjabi poetry, a lot of it composed by him, was truly baffling. So was his knowledge of the scriptures: the Vedas, Upanishads, the Bible, Koran and the Granth Sahib. As a young man, he had been strikingly handsome and acknowledged for his spell-binding oratory. At 86, although confined to his bed, his face has an unearthly glow and his words compel attention. I can well understand why so many people are drawn towards him like iron filings to a magnet. However, I failed to relate to him as I have failed to relate to other charismatic men. I would like to have levelled with him, question him, contradict him, read and criticize his Persian and Urdu poetry, strip him of the aura of sanctity in which he is shrouded. As a mortal, Bhola Nath is a most attractive man. As His Holiness Shri Bhola Nath Ji Maharaj, *Ghulam Roo-e-Zameen,* I found him beyond my reach.

The Hindustan Times, 2 July 1988

■

Deepavali Gods and prayer

There are almost half-a-dozen versions of the origin of Diwali and almost as many gods and goddesses associated with it. It is the day Shri Rama returned to

Ayodhya, the day Vikramaditya was crowned King-Emperor, the day Lord Krishna killed Narakasura, the day Shiva, having lost everything in a gamble to Parvati, had his domain won back for him by his son, Ganapati. But for some obscure reason, the deity most favoured for worship on this auspicious day is Lakshmi, the goddess of wealth. That proves, if any proof were needed, that whatever be our pretensions to spirituality, when it comes to the crunch, it is material prosperity and our account books *(bahee-khatas)* that we worship. I am all for material gains and give a fig for spirituality. I wish my readers more money and better health on this Diwali: happiness follows good health and a healthy bank balance as surely as day follows night.

While living in Maharashtra, I came across yet another version of Diwali. There, they commemorate it as the day when Lord Vishnu deprived Raja Bali of his Kingdom. Maharashtrian women make effigies of Bali and pray, 'May all evil disappear.'

Since there is little likelihood of Bhagwan Vishnu being able or willing to banish all evil for all times to come, I will make my prayer less demanding: 'Please Lord, silence all guns for just one week. If you can't do that all over the world, at least do so in Punjab and Sri Lanka.'

The Hindustan Times, 24 October 1987

Neither Marx nor God

Both God and Karl Marx have disappointed me. I haven't read all that Marx wrote (I doubt if many self-styled Marxists have done so), nor have I read all the praises showered on God in the scriptures of all religions. But I have read enough of both and found them tedious, boring and often inaccurate. Some religious scriptures undoubtedly have a few moving passages, but most of them are repetitive and with little substance. I have also discovered that people who are moved by recitations of scriptures are more hypnotized by the sound of their words than their sense: the more obscure the language the greater its spell-binding power. The more you try to understand their meaning through translations the less you will be impressed by them. Personally I get more out of Kalidas, Shakespeare, Goethe, Ghalib, Tagore, Iqbal and Faiz than I get out of all the religious classics put together.

It is the same with Karl Marx whose death centenary was celebrated all over the world on the 14th of March. I struggled with his *Das Kapital*, found the going too heavy and contented myself with its summary and whatever my then guru, Harold Laski, had to say about it and other Marxist literature. Marx was an atheist and denied the existence of God. He was as wrong as the theists who maintain that there is a God. Agnostics, who take a humbler line, are on firmer ground because they admit that they do not know whether or not God exists. Marx was right in saying that religion is an opiate of the masses. Now, Marxism has also become a religion and, as Vonstein remarked, become an opiate of the asses. Marx was wrong in believing that religion would disappear. Far from disappearing, it has come back into its own with greater vigour all over the world.

Marx erred on many other points. He prophesied a class struggle that would end in the defeat of capitalism and victory for the proletariat. He exhorted workers of the world to rise because they had nothing to lose but their chains. He predicted a dictatorship of the proletariat and the state withering away. None of these prophecies have been fulfilled. Capitalism remains solidly entrenched in many countries. Privately-owned enterprises have proved to be more efficient than state-owned enterprises and more benign in their dealings with their workers. In capitalist countries, workers are free to form labour unions and strike for their rights. In communist countries, they are not. The travails of Poland's Solidarity are eloquent testimony of Marxist dreams of a workers' paradise turning into a nightmare.

In what communist country has the state withered away? None. Most are as dictatorial as Hitlerite Germany. They have concentration camps where inhuman tortures are practised. In the Fatherland of the Communists, Soviet Russia, there is discrimination against ethnic minorities like the Jews. No country in the world today can match the Soviet Union's record of swallowing other countries. World War II brought the Baltic states and Poland within its orbit. Independence movements in Czechoslovakia and Hungary were crushed brutally. And three years ago, without any provocation or excuse, the Soviets invaded Afghanistan and have for all practical purposes annexed it. Poor Marx, who was born a Jew, must be turning in his grave.

However, to be fair to him, Karl Marx did rouse the conscience of the world against the exploitation of labour, of the need to provide equal opportunities to all citizens and to give people the control of the means of production. It is the Marxists who have given Karl Marx a bad name. They have earned notoriety for shirking work (*kaamchors*). Will Rogers was right in his opinion that if communists worked as hard as they talked, they'd have the most prosperous government in the world. But with them it is one-third practice and two-thirds explanation. Ebenezer Elliot's definition of a communist is apt:

What is a communist? One who has yearnings
For an equal division of unequal earnings,
Idler or bungler, or both, he is willing
To fork out his penny and pocket your shilling.
                          The Hindustan Times, 3 April 1983

■

Let us clean our temples

By coincidence, most of my travels over the last two years took me to many places of pilgrimage—Hindu, Muslim and Sikh—all over the country. I was angered by the atmosphere that prevails, the large number of people who make their living by parasiting on hapless pilgrims, and the total absence of an aura of sanctity that I naively expected to see. It struck me that religious parasitism is a phenomenon of the Indo-Gangetic plain; one sees much less of it in the Deccan and the South. Though mosques and gurudwaras are free of agents of religious organizations and keep beggars outside sacred premises, corruption and misuse of offerings are a common practice. There is little to choose between Sufi *dargahs* like those of Hazrat Moinuddin Chisti in Ajmer and Nizamuddin Auliya in New Delhi and historic Hindu temples such as Vaishno Devi in Jammu; those in Mathura, Vrindavan, Badrinath, Hardwar, Allahabad and Varanasi in UP; Lingaraj and Jagannath in Orissa and the Kali temple in Calcutta. All of them have as many beggars as worshippers and everywhere you go you are accosted by men armed with receipt books asking for donations for some charity or the other. And without exception they are ill-maintained, squalid and filthy.

The most sinister freemasonry is that of the *pandas* who fatten on pilgrims' religious susceptibilities. My first experience of them was almost 50 years ago at Hardwar. I had taken my grandmother's ashes to be

immersed in the Ganga. I was immediately collared
by a pot-bellied gentleman who claimed to be my
family *panda*. He led me to the river bank, took the
little sack of ashes from my hand and began to pour
the contents on a dry step and slowly push the ashes
into the river with his feet. I was appalled at such
irreverence to my grandmother's remains and protested
loudly. He ignored me and drowned my protestations
by loudly chanting *mantras*. (The foot-search was to
locate any pieces of gold or silver from the dead person's
teeth that might have been cremated with the body.)
Then I noticed a number of boys standing waist-deep
in the river reflecting glass mirrors into the water. The
sun's rays thus deflected would catch the glitter of silver
or gold. I was so incensed that I wanted to push my
panda and all the urchins into the swift-flowing stream.
It was shameless robbery of the dead. The practice
continues unabated. I continue to visit Hardwar at least
once a year to watch the worship of the Ganga at sunset,
but will never again let the ashes of a friend or a relation
be treated in the manner my grandmother's were.

My last two pilgrimages were to the Lingaraj temple
in Bhubaneswar and the Jagannath temple at Puri. I
had been to Lingaraj earlier but wanted to show my
wife the beautiful sculpture on its main sanctum. The
temple complex has over a dozen smaller shrines.
Outside each was a tray full of currency notes and
coins and a *panda* pleading with every passerby to
make an offering. If you put something in their hands,
you were blessed. If you did not, they passed rude

remarks. The inner sanctum was more like a vegetable market than a place of worship. The corridor was very poorly lit, the ground slippery with the slime of coconut juice: I am sure many worshippers must have sprained their ankles or fractured their bones falling on the hard floor. Round the *lingum* was a scene of unbelievable pandemonium as *pandas* grabbed offerings in return for flowers or *sindoor*. There was none of the solemnity one expects in a place of worship.

The temple of Jagannath at Puri probably receives as many if not more worshippers than the Meenakshi temple at Madurai. The Madurai temple is cleaner and has no priests pursuing pilgrims. At Puri they begin to close round you half a mile away from the temple and do not leave you till they have extracted whatever you have in cash on your person. It can be a harrowing experience. And the inner sanctum where Jagannath, Subhadra and Balaram are enshrined is again totally lacking in decorum; the slime on the floor makes the *parikrama* a hazardous exercise.

Why is it that while most *ashrams* are clean and well-maintained, most temples are far from being either clean or properly looked after? The government is unlikely to put its hand in this hornet's nest of vested interests; it has to be some Hindu voluntary organization which should take it upon itself to restore the sanctity of our temples.

Sunday, 25 March 1989

■

Sati and Hindu-Sikh psyche

The self-immolation by the 18-year-old Roop Kanwar near Jaipur once again demonstrates that there are two kinds of Indians, and the gulf that separates them remains to be bridged. On the one side is the vast majority which still harbours respect for the widow who ceremoniously mounts her husband's funeral pyre. They applaud her as the paradigm of supreme sacrifice, deify her as the reincarnation of a goddess and raise temples to her memory. On the other side is the minority of modern, Westernized Indians who decry the act as barbarous and call upon the administration to hand out deterrent punishment to those who collaborated in it. They get more publicity because of a like-minded media. But if they think that *sati*-supporters are a lunatic fringe who will soon be wiped out, they are in for many unpleasant surprises.

Self-immolation by widows will continue because reverence for them is too deep-rooted in our psyches to be completely eradicated. All over northern India are umbrella-shaped (*chhatree*) *sati* monuments bearing witness to an unbroken tradition of widow-immolation. Amongst certain tribes like the Rajputs there was pressure of a time-honoured custom, a kind of *noblesse oblige* which made the practice obligatory. If the widow was reluctant to end her life, she was drugged and pushed onto the burning pyre. The practice was by no means confined to the Rajputs. When the Jat Sikh Maharajah, Ranjit Singh, died, seven of his *ranis* and concubines were cremated with him. The practice was followed at the cremation of his son, Kharak Singh.

Lord William Bentinck made *sati* a crime and succeeded in reducing its incidence. He was never able to fully suppress it, much less exorcize it from the Hindu-Sikh psyche. Even I who condemn *sati* as a remnant of medieval barbarity feel a glow of pride when I read of Rajput women committing *jauhar* rather than surrendering themselves to a victorious enemy. *Sati* is only a singular manifestation of the mass *jauhar* mentality.

It remains a man's world. No one has ever heard of a man mounting the funeral pyre of his dead wife and becoming a *sata*. No, the first thing he does—and often before he returns home from his wife's cremation—is to entertain a proposal for another wife. In my village it used to be customary for everyone returning from a funeral to have a bath at the well before entering their homes. At the time, any man who wanted to give his daughter to the widower would pick up his wet undergarment (*kachha*) as a form of proposal. It was as cold blooded as that.

How can you fight a sentiment that has religious sanction and has been nourished over the centuries! Refresh your religious memory. The word *sati* means true. Sati was the daughter of sage Daksha and the beloved of Lord Siva whom her father hated. At her *swayamvara*, Siva, who had not been invited, came floating through the air and got the matrimonial garland flung by Sati round his neck. Daksha never forgave Siva for becoming his son-in-law and refused to invite him to a sacrificial feast. That was enough for Sati to hurl herself into a *jwalamukhi* (volcano).

Thereafter legends vary. Some say Sati was changed into a *koel*; others claim that she was reborn as Goddess Uma. Yet others hold that Siva danced round the world seven times with her charred body and restored her to life. It is also believed by some people that Lord Vishnu (the preserver), fearing that Siva might become too powerful, cut up Sati's body into many pieces; wherever pieces of her limbs fell became a *peethasthana*—a place of pilgrimage. They can be found all over India.

Why Hindu-Sikh women have allowed such discrimination in the code of conduct on the demise of their spouses is beyond me. They have in fact accepted *sati* as the most befitting end to their lives. Has it ever occurred to you that in nine out of ten cases of suicides committed by Hindu-Sikh married women, the death is caused by burn rather than by poison, strangulation, drowning or being run over by railway trains? Why? Because burning is *sati*; other forms of death are not.

Sunday, 17 October 1987

■

Worship of the Ganga

Of all the rivers of the world, none has received as much adoration as the Ganga. Though there is scant reference to it in the Vedas, it assumes a dominant position in the Puranas. She is the daughter of Himavat, the Himalayas, and Mena, the sister of Parvati, wife of Siva. Originally, the river was confined to the realms of paradise. When brought to earth to irrigate barren land, it came down in such a mighty torrent that it would have drowned everything but for Siva breaking its downfall on his head and allowing it to flow out into seven streams, *Sapta Sindhava*—the seven sacred rivers of India, the most sacred being the Ganga.

No one knows why or when Ganga's waters acquired powers of healing minds and bodies. But long before records started being kept, men who were disillusioned with life or were in search of eternal truths gave up other pursuits to retire into caves in valleys through which the Ganga ran to meditate in the silence of mountain fastnesses. At dawn, they stood in the icy-cold waters of the river to welcome the rising sun. At sunset, they floated leaf boats with flowers and oil lamps on its fast-moving streams.

Waters of the Ganga acquired the reputation of healing properties. They were undoubtedly the cleanest, clearest source of potable water near Delhi and Agra which were for centuries the seats of rulers of India. The 14th century ruler at Delhi, Mohammed bin Tughlaq, organized a regular supply of drinking water from Hardwar for inmates of his palace. The practice was followed from one dynasty to the next. The Mughal emperor Akbar drank only Ganga water and ordered it to be used in the royal kitchen. Though

Muslims attached no religious significance to it, the Ganga found an important place in their thinking. Allama Iqbal, one of the founding fathers of Pakistan and the greatest Urdu poet of his times, had this to say:

Ai aab-e-rood-e-Ganga,
Voh din hai yaad tujh ko
Utra terey kinaarey
Jab kaarvaan hamaara?
(O, limpid waters of the Ganga,
remember you the day,
When our caravan stopped by your banks
And forever came to stay?)

For the Hindus, *Ganga jal* (Ganga water) has more spiritual than mundane significance. A newborn babe has a few drops put in its mouth. So has a dying person before he breathes his last. A dip in the river washes away all sins. Ashes of the dead are immersed in it.

The water of the Ganga is in great demand all over the country. As you go along the road to Hardwar, you pass long lines of *kanwarias* carrying pots containing *Ganga jal* slung on poles. At short distances, there are small platforms for them to rest their cargo, as the pots must never touch the ground. In Calcutta, there are *jal yatris*, water pilgrims. Soon after Shivratri, they can be seen taking water pots from the Tribeni in Howrah district, to the Tarakeshwar temple in Hooghly district, calling out *Baba Tarakeshwari serai nomo*

(obeisance and service to Baba Tarakeshwari), or
Bholey Baba paar karega (Lord Shiva will take you
across) or simply, *Bom, bom bholey, Taraknath boley
bom bom.*

The Ganga is sacred from its source, Gangotri, down
the mountains past Rudraprayag, Devprayag,
Badrinath and Rishikesh till it enters the plains at
Hardwar. So far it is a fast-moving river, crystal clear
and sparkling. After Hardwar, it slows down. By the
time it reaches Allahabad for its *sangam* (confluence
with the Yamuna), it becomes a sluggish stretch of
water full of human garbage. It continues to gather
debris as it goes past Benares and Patna to its junction
with the mighty Brahmaputra to become the Hooghly
and empty itself in the Bay of Bengal.

On its long journey from the Himalayas to the sea,
many rivers join it while canals rob it of its waters. It
is a strange phenomenon that though the water from
the main stream is regarded sacred, the same water
running in canals and taps is accorded no sanctity.
Even in the places of pilgrimage, some small areas
along the bank are more sacred than others. In
Hardwar, *Har-ki-Paudi* (Footsteps of the Lord), a 50-
yard stretch on the right bank of the river, is about the
most sacred place in India. Here, pilgrims throng in
thousands from early hours of the dawn to late at night,
to bathe, pray, make offerings and ask for favours. A
never-to-be-forgotten sight is the *aarti*, worship with
oil lamps, which takes places every evening at sunset.

Hardwar is a comfortable four-hour drive from

Delhi. However, it is advisable to choose an appropriate time of the year for the visit. The best time is from January to April, preferably around Holi, when the countryside en route and the hills around Hardwar are ablaze with the Flame of the Forest and the Coral. Choose a couple of days before the full moon and plan to spend at least one night in the town. It has plenty of hotels, small and big, *ashrams* and *dharamshalas*, lodges to suit your pocket. The menu everywhere is strictly vegetarian; there is also prohibition, but soda water is available and no one really bothers if you enjoy your drink in your room.

A short halt at a midway eatery, *Cheetal Grand*, outside village Khatauli, is a must. It is laid out in a spacious, well-kept garden. Large cages with roosters, ducks, geese, turkeys and guinea fowl call and cackle all day long. The service is fast, the food of gourmet quality. The owner, Urooj Nisar, does good business: he feeds upto 8,000 guests every day. It is a meeting place for people taking the ashes of their loved ones to immerse in the Ganga at Hardwar and those returning after having done so. It is also the favourite picnic spot for boys and girls from schools in Mussoorie, Dehra Dun, Hardwar and Ranipur.

Make sure you get to the *ghat* (embankment) well before sunset. Stroll along the banks of the river and you will meet many well-fed cows, ash-smeared *sadhus* smoking *ganja* and opium in their *chillums*. Every few yards, there will be a conclave of men and women— many more women than men—listening to *purvachans* being delivered to some holy personage. In Hardwar, holy men are nine to a dozen. So are *pandas* who can trace your lineage back to forefathers you have never heard of—for a fee. Also, men with receipt books asking for donations for *gaushalas* (cattle pens) and other worthy causes. Avoid them.

As the sun goes down over the range of hills in the west, a deep shade falls over Hardwar and the silvery moonlight takes over. It is time to find a vantage point from where you can see the *aarti*. There is a bridge along the right bank to an island facing *Har-ki-Paudi* on which stands a clock tower. The bridge and the island give a splendid view of what is going on at *Har-ki-Paudi* where the action takes place. Most pilgrims prefer to sit on the steps along *Har-ki-Paudi* just above the stream because it is there that *pandas* take offerings from them. In return, they give them leaf boats full of flowers and lit oil lamps, and invoke the blessings of Mother Ganga—all for a fee.

Hardwar has hundreds of temples lining the bank, but not one of them of any architectural pretensions. Evening shadows envelop their ugliness and the skullduggery of *pandas* looting gullible pilgrims. Only the Ganga remains as pure as the snows which give it birth. Bathed in early moonlight, it assumes ethereal beauty. Suddenly, a cry goes up, *Bolo, bolo Ganga Mata Ki*, and thousands of voices yell in triumph *Jai*—victory of the Mother Ganga. The *aarti* is about to begin. All the steps leading to and around *Har-ki-Paudi*, the bridge and the clock-tower island are crammed with pilgrims and sightseers.

Men start striking gongs with mallets: this is in honour of the lesser gods. Then, bells of temples start clanging. Men holding candelabras with dozens of oil lamps each, stand ankle-deep in the river and wave them over it. Conch shells are blown. Leaf boats with flowers and *diyas* bob up and down the fast-moving current and disappear from view. Above all this cacophony of light and the din of gongs and bells, rises the chant:

Om, Jai Gangey Mata
(Victory to Mother Ganga)

The spectacle lasts barely ten minutes. It transports you to another world. It will haunt you for the rest of your nights and days.

■

Watching Nature

How it all began

Many years ago when I was a young man, I happened to spend a summer with my friends, the Wints, in Oxford. Guy Wint was on the staff of *The Observer* and was away in London most of the day. His wife, Freda, had converted to Buddhism and was also out most of the time meeting fellow Buddhists. Their son, Ben, was at a boarding school. For company, I had the Wints' three-year-old daughter, Allegra. In the mornings, I worked in my room.

When Allegra returned from her nursery school, I gave her a sandwich and a glass of milk before we went out for a walk. Since she knew the neighbourhood, she led the way along paths running through woods of oak, beech and rhododendron to the University cricket grounds. I would watch the game for a while—the Nawab of Pataudi often played there—buy her an ice-cream and then follow her back homewards.

Allegra, or Leggie as we called her, was a great chatterbox as well as an avid collector of wild flowers. Our return journey always took much longer as I had to pick whatever flower she wanted. She would point in some direction and order: 'I want those snow-drops behind that bush.' Or shout, 'Goody! I want them blue-bells! I want lots of them for Mummy!' Then there were periwinkles and lilies-of-the-valley, and many others.

By the time we had our hands full of flowers, Leggie was too tired to leg it home. I had to go down on my knees for her to climb up on my shoulders. She had her legs round my neck and her chin resting on my head. A game she enjoyed was to stick flowers in my turban and beard. By the time we got home, I looked like a wild man of the woods. It was from little Allegra Wint that I learnt the names of many English wild flowers.

On weekends when the Wint family was at home, we spent most of the day sunning ourselves in the garden. Since the Wints had a few cherry and apple trees, there were lots of birds in their garden. The dawn chorus was opened by thrushes and blackbirds. They sang through the day till late into the twilight. Both birds sounded exactly alike to me. Freda would quote Robert Browning to explain the difference:

That's the wise thrush; he sings each song twice over,
Lest you should think he never could recapture
The first fine careless rapture.

*

What perhaps accounts for the profusion of bird life in our locality are several nurseries in the vicinity, the foliage of many old *papari (Pongamia glabra)* trees and bushes of cannabis sativa *(bhaang)* which grow wild. I have not kept a count of the variety of birds that frequent my garden but there is never a time when there are none. Also, there are lots of butterflies, beetles, wasps, ants, bees and bugs of different kinds.

There was a time when I spent Sunday mornings in winter in the countryside armed with a pair of binoculars and Salim Ali's or Whistler's books on Indian birds. My favourite haunts were the banks of the Jamuna behind Tilpat village; Surajkund, the dam which supplies water to its pool; and the ruins of Tughlaqabad Fort with its troops of rhesus monkeys. I still manage to visit these places at least once a year to renew acquaintance with water fowl, skylarks, weaver birds and variety of wild plants like *akk, debla, vasicka,* mesquite, Mexican poppy and lantana which grow in profusion all round Delhi.

*

The wise thrushes of Oxford had not read Browning and rarely repeated their notes. Or perhaps the blackbirds deliberately went over theirs again to confuse people like me. Then there were chaffinches, buntings, white throats, and many other varieties of birds whose songs became familiar to me. That summer, I heard nightingales on the Italian lakes and in the forest of Fontainebleau. (Contrary to the popular notion, nightingales sing at all hours of the day and night.)

Back home in Delhi, I felt as if I was on alien territory as far as the fauna and the flora were concerned. Before I had gone abroad, I had taken no interest in nature. When I returned I felt acutely conscious of this lacuna in my information as I could not identify more than a couple of dozen birds or trees.

Getting to know about them was tedious but immensely rewarding.

I acquired books on trees, birds and insects and spent my spare time identifying those I did not know. I sought the company of bird-watchers and horticulturists. Gradually my fund of information increased, and I dared to give talks on Delhi's natural phenomena on All India Radio and Doordarshan.

For the last many years I have maintained a record of the natural phenomena I encounter every day. However, my nature-watching is done in a very restricted landscape, most of it in my private back garden. It is a small rectangular plot of green enclosed on two adjacent sides by a barbed wire fence covered over by bougainvillea creepers of different hues. The other two sides are formed by my neighbour's and my own apartments. He has fenced himself off by a wall of hibiscus; I have four ten-year-old avocado trees (perhaps the only ones in Delhi) which between them yield no more than a dozen pears every monsoon season; and a tall eucalyptus smothered by a purple bougainvillea.

There is a small patch of grass with some limes, oranges, grapefruits and a pomegranate. I do not grow many flowers; a bush of gardenia, a couple of jasmines and a Queen of the Night (*Raat ki Rani*). Since my wife has strictly utilitarian views on gardening, most of what we have is reserved for growing vegetables. At the farther end of this little garden I have placed a bird bath which is shared by sparrows, crows, mynahs, kites, pigeons, babblers and a dozen stray cats which have made my home theirs.

Facing my apartment on the front side is a squarish lawn shared by other residents of Sujan Singh Park. It has several large trees of the ficus family, a young choryzzia and an old mulberry. I have a view of this lawn from my sitting room windows framed by a *madhumalati* creeper and a hedge of hibiscus.

The Hindustan Times, 7 April 1990

■

Mango fool

There is nothing foolish about mango fool. On the contrary, when mangoes are not up to the mark they are expected to be, all you have to do is to pulp them, add judicious measures of cream and sugar, cool the mix in a freezer and—*voila*—you have a sweet dish which puts the best fruit cocktails doused with maraschino to shame.

For those of us who live in the north-western part of the country, June is the real mango month. But ever since rail and air transport was pressed into service, we start the mango season in March and extend it to October. There are over 100 varieties of mangoes grown all over the country—half of India's trees are mango trees. Some variety or the other is airlifted to the capital from early spring. By the end of April, the most highly rated Alfonso, grown around Ratnagiri on the Konkan coast of Maharashtra, is available in Delhi—at a price few can pay. It is rightly known as 'the magic lamp' to be presented to people in power from whom you expect favours. Andhra has its own variety best suited for bribery, known as the Imam Pasand (the Imam's choice) as well as 'Collector Sahib'. Pandit Nehru's favourite was the Dussehri, grown in and around the orchards of Malihabad in Uttar Pradesh. He used to send a crate of Dussehris to Queen Elizabeth every summer. My favourite remains the Langra (Lame), so named after a lame fakir of Delhi. There are lots of Langra orchards around Delhi, but the most succulent varieties come from Uttar Pradesh. It has a slightly 'turpentiney' flavour and is not recommended for those who have sensitive throats. Equally tasty are the Chausa, Rataul and the new hybrid, Amrapalli. Whatever be your favourite, do not consume more than two or at the most three a day. Mangoes are highly laxative: *do ya teen, bas!*

I am not sure how the mango evolved. The fruit bears remarkable resemblance to the fruit of the neem tree, *niboli*. When ripe yellow, it looks like a miniature mango and the texture of its pulp, though not the same taste, is like that of a mango. If it is an evolution of the *niboli*, it must have taken place a million years ago. Certainly by the time of Kalidasa, the mango had evolved into its fullness, because the poet goes lyrical over it. Alexander the Great, the Chinese pilgrim Hieun Tsang and the Moor, Ibn Batuta, all relished it. Though

Babar thought it was highly overrated, his grandson, Akbar, planted an extensive orchard of 1,00,000 trees in Darbhanga, known thereafter as Lakhi Bagh.

Indians' love for mangoes surpasses the Arabs' love for dates or the central Asians' love for watermelons and Kandahar grapes. Mughal emperors and ladies of their harems invested their wealth in mango orchards. Bahadur Shah Zafar, the last of the august line, whose domain did not extend beyond the walls of Shahjahanabad, had some of the best varieties planted in the squarish garden in the Red Fort known as Hayat Baksh (Life Giving). Delhi's most celebrated poet, Asadullah Khan Ghalib, was addicted to mangoes and shamelessly sponged on his royal master. Once when strolling with his patron in Hayat Baksh, he is reported to have said, 'Your Majesty, I am told that every mango bears the name of the person it is meant for on its seed-stone. I wonder if any of these growing in your garden have Ghalib's name imprinted on them.'

Another poet-lover of mangoes who did not hesitate to ask for them was Akbar Ilahabadi. Once he wrote to a friend who owned a large orchard:

Neither letter nor message from my
beloved send to me.
If you must send something this season,
mangoes let them be.
Make sure there are some that I can keep
to eat another day,
If twenty are ripe add another ten that

can stay.
Your slave's address you know, it remains
the same
Despatch them to Allahabad in a parcel
with my name.
Whatever you do, in your reply
please be not so brash
'Order for mangoes received:
First send
the cash.'

Sunday, 9 June 1990

■

Songs of the monsoon

Come June and my ears are wide open to catch the
melancholy, wailing cry of the pied-crested cuckoo,
the harbinger of the monsoon known to us as the *megha
papeeha* (Clamator Jacobinus). For many years I have
recorded in my diary the date when I first heard it in
summer. It is usually around the middle of June. By
the end of May the monsoon hits the coast of Kerala; a
few days later it spreads over the Konkan coast; Bombay
usually expects its first heavy downpour on the 9th of
June. By then, the *megha papeeha* is well on its way
towards the Indo-Gangetic plains. Last year I heard it
on the 8th of June and prophesied that in ten days, the
monsoon would reach Delhi. It didn't. The *papeeha*

(hawk cuckoo or the brain-fever bird) cried incessantly, but the *megha papeeha* was heard for a few days and then fell silent. There was hardly any rain.

The monsoon remains the most memorable experience of our lives. Lives of more than half the people of the world living in Asia, Australia and Africa are affected by its vagaries. And yet we know very little about it. What really causes it is the reversal of wind direction between summer and winter. In the summer they blow inland from the cooler oceans towards the warmer landmass; in winter from the cold of the land towards the warmer oceans.

The celebrated astronomer, Halley, drew a wind chart as early as 1688 AD, and explained that the primary cause of the annual cycle of the monsoon circulation was the differential between ocean and land caused by the seasonal march of the sun. Differential heating caused differences in atmospheric air pressure which had to be equalized by winds blowing from high pressure to lower pressure zones.

Like the pied-crested cuckoo, Arab seamen were the first to take advantage of favourable winds to get to India and return with their dhows laden with Indian silks and spices when the monsoons were over. It was Arab seamen who disclosed to the Portuguese mariner, Vasco da Gama, the secrets of navigation between east Africa and India and opened up India to the Europeans.

While coastal areas and north-eastern regions are already experiencing the monsoon, we in the hinterland suffer the pre-monsoon heat and dust so vividly described by Kipling:

> No hope, no change! The clouds have shut us in
> And through the cloud the sullen sun strikes down
> Full on the bosom of the tortured town,
> Till night falls heavy as remembered sin
> That will not suffer sleep or thought of ease,
> And, hour on hour, the dry-eyed moon in spite
> Glares through the haze and mocks with watery light
> The torment of the uncomplaining trees,
> Far off, the thunder bellows her despair
> To echoing earth, thrice parched.
> The lightnings fly
> In vain. No help the heaped-up clouds afford.
> But wearier weight of burdened, burning air,
> What truce with dawn? Look, from the aching sky
> Day stalks, a tyrant with a flaming sword!

It won't be too long a wait now. How beautifully
Amaru (9th century AD) captured the onset of the
monsoon:

> At night the rain came, and the thunder deep
> Rolled in the distance; and he could not sleep
> But tossed and turned, with long and frequent sighs,
> And as he listened, tears came to his eyes;
> And thinking of his young wife left alone,
> He sobbed and wept aloud until the dawn.
> And from that time on
> The villagers made it a strict rule that no traveller

Should be allowed to take a room for the night in the village.

The monsoon brought the best out of our poets. Perhaps the most memorable lines in Tagore's *Gitanjali* are on the rains:

Clouds heap upon clouds and it darkens
Ah, love, why dost thou let me wait outside at the door all alone?
In the busy moments of the noontide work I am with the crowd,
But on this dark lonely day it is only for thee I hope
If thou showest me not thy face, if thou leavest me
Wholly aside, I know not how I am to pass these long, rainy hours.
I keep gazing on the far-away gloom of the sky
And my heart wanders wailing with the restless wind.

Sunday, 2 July 1988

■

Dog control

I am a dog lover living among cats. I have reared dozens of kittens in my lap but cannot call even one of them my friend. They are grabbers who give you nothing in return. They have no conversation except purring when sponging on me. On the other hand, I had a German shepherd called Simba who was a great communicator. I haven't had another dog since Simba died over 20 years ago. It is easier to replace a dead wife with a new one, but replacing a dog who was your best friend with another is an act of gross disloyalty.

There are some people who love all animals and others who hate all of them. Animal haters are a subhuman species and should be ostracized from society. I love animal lovers. One of them is Diana Ratnagar of *Beauty Without Cruelty,* based in Pune. She is a young and pretty Bawaji (Parsee) whose life's mission is to eliminate animal suffering.

The principal causes for inflicting pain on animals are man-manipulated propagation of a species for economic exploitation and unchecked natural increase of another. The best examples of the first are the propagation of crocodiles and Karakul lambs. They are reared in farms away from predators provided by nature to keep their population under control. Then men slaughter them to make money from their skins. Prime examples of unchecked natural increase are cats, dogs and cattle. When they increase beyond control, some have to be destroyed. Dogs, for example, multiply according to the Malthusian formula. A bitch over a year old litters every six months bearing an average of six puppies. In three years, between her and her progeny, they can produce over 340 dogs. In unhygienic conditions, the incidence of rabies becomes very high. All municipalities employ dog killers who use the most inhuman methods to trap and destroy them. Now a breakthrough has been achieved by which we can keep dog (and other mammal) populations under control without inflicting pain or killing them. Prof G.P. Talwar and Dr Anil Suri have between them produced a serum aptly named 'Talsur', which when injected into a male dog, sterilizes it for life. Used extensively, it will dramatically bring down our canine population. The injection has no side effects on the animal. We are not sure how it will affect the female of the species. A bitch on heat which has only impotent dogs sniffing at her posterior may turn savage. It was too delicate a question for me to pose to anyone as prim and proper as Diana Ratnagar.

The Hindustan Times, 26 December 1987

■

Burial more patriotic than cremation

In an extempore appearance on Doordarshan a few days ago, I was questioned mainly on two topics: population explosion and fouling of the environment. I was allowed to say that if an epidemic wiped out half our population, it might prove to be a boon in disguise because India can afford to feed, clothe, educate and house 400 million people; it cannot do the same for 800 million people. Most of our present-day problems of violence and corruption are due to the fact that we are too many with not enough to go around for all of us. About environment I was allowed to say that if we continue to destroy our forests at the pace we are doing, by the end of the century, we will have reduced our country to a desert. *Vanamahotsavas* organized by governmental agencies have become a ritual when ministers and officials can have themselves photographed planting saplings. If our forests are to be revived, tree-planting and their survival have to become people's movements. Meanwhile, laws should be enacted to ban the use of wood for furniture (there are plenty of substitutes available) and newspapers forbidden from using more than a prescribed number of pages. One suggestion that I was most eager to air, I was requested not to, as it might be taken as coming from the government and thus prejudice the chances of the ruling party's candidates in the by-elections. I would like to put it across as forcefully as I can in this column.

Is there anything in the Hindu Dharma which prescribes that the dead must be cremated? I don't think so. I know of many Hindu communities in the South which bury their dead. M.G. Ramachandran, and before him Annadorai, both Hindus, were buried. Many Jain Munis are buried. What then is wrong if all our big cities provided Hindu-Sikh burial grounds for those who wish to opt for them rather than have tonnes of precious wood destroyed in the process? These need not be like Christian or Muslim cemeteries which occupy precious land around all our cities, but unique in forbidding the use of tombstones. Just bury the dead next to the earth and give back the soil of our Motherland from which we took so much, something of what remains of us to enrich it. Every five years or so, run a tractor over the graveyard and plant fruit trees or vegetables in it. If there was such a non-communal burial ground, I would gladly opt for it rather than make some tree commit sati over my body.

The Hindustan Times, 25 June 1988

■

Billo

My granddaughter Naina found a kitten lying on the road. It had been bitten and mauled by a dog and left for dead. It was in a state of shock. She brought it home and nursed it for several weeks, cradling it in her arms like a new-born baby. Its face had been cut and one eye damaged seemingly beyond repair.

Slowly the kitten recovered. Its wound healed and its damaged eye recovered its golden sparkle. But it is scared to go out of the flat because of the dogs. Since my granddaughter has to be at the university for several hours of the day, it attached itself to her maid-servant, Kamla.

During the day, it remains close to Kamla and when my granddaughter comes back, it shuttles between the two, purring as it snuggles in their laps. When neither of her two foster mothers is at home, it sits in my ailing wife's lap and purrs louder to give her comfort. It refuses to respond to my overtures.

When I put it in my lap, it stops purring and is impatient to get away. It hurts my pride, because I am convinced all animals like me as much as I like them. I didn't know whether it is female or male—a *billee* or a *billa*, so I have named it 'Billo'. Cats do not respond to names; neither does Billo.

Billo has grown into a full-sized cat and spends most of its time in my apartment without coming too close to me except when I am having my meals. Then, it tries to grab whatever it can lay its paws or mouth on and runs away. It looks for things under sofas and chairs, examines all my bookshelves and artefacts and is particularly intrigued by the TV set.

Early one morning, when without switching on the lights I switched on the TV, I noticed a long tail dangling in front of the screen. It was Billo seated on the top surveying the room. As the sound came on, it went round the set looking for its source. Then it stared at the pictures and pawed the screen to make sure if the flattened images were of real people.

For many days the TV set became its favourite perch. Then one day as I was watching Discovery Channel, its hackles went up as a tiger appeared on the screen. The tiger roared and Billo fled for its life. Since then, it has not been near the TV set.

Not all people like cats. Some have even gone to the extent of wanting to pass laws to prevent them from wandering about. The classic example is of the state of Illinois considering a bill to ban their prowling about.

When it came for approval to Adelai Stevenson, Governor of the state, he wrote a dissenting note: 'I cannot agree that it should be the declared public policy of Illinois that a cat visiting a neighbour's yard or crossing the highway is a public nuisance. It is in the nature of cats to do a certain amount of unescorted roaming—to escort a cat on a leash is against the nature of the owners.

'Moreover, cats perform useful service, particularly in the rural areas. The problem of the cat versus the bird or the rat is as old as time. If we attempt to resolve it by legislation, who knows but what we may be called upon to take sides as well as on the age-old problems of dog versus cat, bird versus bird, or even bird versus worm. In my opinion, the state of Illinois and its local government bodies already have enough to do without trying to control feline delinquency.'

There must be something in my character which Billo does not like. Perhaps like Maneka Gandhi and a few others of her kind, Billo has come to the conclusion that I am not a nice man to know.

The Hindustan Times, 22 December 2001

Traveller's Tales

Spanning Kaushalya

Everytime I went up the Kalka-Shimla road, I used to stop at a densely wooded spot in the hope of catching a glimpse of the Paradise Fly Catchers which nested in the thick cluster of bamboo groves. I rarely saw them. But the spot had more to it then these silver-n-snow-white birds with long tapering tails. Across the valley was a mountain shaped very much like a woman's breast. And atop it like a nipple sat a dilapidated fortress built by the Gorkhas. Apparently they had spread their arms westward from Nepal till they were checked by the combined forces of the hill Rajputs and the Sikhs. They abandoned this post sometime in the 1830s. It still bears the name of a neighbouring village, Garhi Banasar.

Besides the Gorkha fortress which I always promised myself I would visit one day, the entire hillside was terraced with fields growing paddy, corn, potatoes and other vegetables. Just as I couldn't get to the other side except by taking a 50-mile jeepable track, so the peasants of the hundreds of villages lying below the fortress could not get their produce to the markets in the plains without trudging 5,000 feet downhill into the valley through which flowed the Kaushalya on its way to its *sangam* with the Ghaggar, and then uphill another 2,000 feet to get on to the Kalka-Shimla road. It was a spine-breaking journey, taking a whole day. By the time they reached Kalka, their vegetables had gone stale and they got very little for them. Only if someone could span the valley of the Kaushalya by a rope bridge, the whole aspect of the hillside would change. No individual could undertake the task. I hoped someday the State Government would do the job.

It was not the Himachal Government but a Himachali from Sarhan village who made this dream a reality. Ramesh Kumar Garg did not take his degree because he was drawn into the family's timber business. In 1977 he visited Switzerland and saw cable cars going from one mountain top to another. Back home, he acquired contractual rights to the pine forests on either side of the Kaushalya. First he built an attractive hotel, Timber Trail, on the Kalka-Shimla highway. Then he built another on the other side of the valley 2,000 feet above his first hotel and named it Timber Trail Heights. Then he connected the two by cable car 1½ kilometres long (the longest in the country). The entire equipment consisting of steel pylons and four steel rope cables was produced in India by Usha Breco of Calcutta. The cable car trip has become a must for people of Chandigarh, Patiala and Ambala—and anyone going up to the Shimla Hills. The enterprise cost Garg Rs 3 crore. It is going to cost him more as the cable cars have developed a wobble and the service has been suspended until they are put right. I am not sure how long it will take him to recover his investment, but I do know that he has brought prosperity to thousands of Himachali peasants who now take their produce across the valley by carriage ropeway in eight minutes

instead of 18 hours. The evidence is here for anyone to
see: new farmsteads with electric lighting and TV
antennae. From the hotel at Banasar you get a
spectacular view of the Kaushalya and the Ghaggar,
the plains of Haryana and Punjab, the Sukhna lake
and the Union Territory of Chandigarh. Himachal could
do with more Himachalis like Ramesh Garg.
Shabaash!

The Hindustan Times, 11 June 1988

■

As others see us

When you read this piece I will be in Bali—perhaps
watching Balinese temple dancers and wondering
whether it is nicer being abroad than in the murky
atmosphere of Delhi. When at home, I make it a point
to get away at least once a month to distance myself
from the capital, to gauge people's opinion of the
administration and also do a bit of *Bharat darshaning.*
Likewise, once or twice a year, I like to get away from
Bharat to get things in clearer focus and also find out
what others think of us. I recommend both exercises to
anyone who has the time and money to spare.

The first thing you discover when abroad is that
foreigners are as little concerned about India as we
Indians are about them. That no longer surprises or
disappoints me. Everyone is more involved with what

is happening in their own village, town, city, state or country than what is going on a thousand miles away. What depresses me more than foreigners' indifference towards India is that the small minority which does interest itself in other countries has a very poor opinion of our conduct in international affairs and an even poorer one of our countrymen who live and work among them. It is a notorious fact that our relations with all our immediate neighbours—Pakistan, China, Nepal, Bangladesh and Sri Lanka—are strained. That should restrain our spokesmen from tendering unsought advice on good neighbourliness to other nations. But our leaders never seem to be able to resist the temptation of preaching to others what they do not practise themselves. Nobody takes them very seriously any more.

Our countrymen abroad also do not enjoy the respect or affection of the community in which they live. They have the reputation of being clannish, cunning, grabbing, ill-mannered and inconsiderate. It is an unfortunate fact that wherever Indians are found in sizeable numbers, they generate anti-Indian feeling. I know this to be true of Europe, Canada, the United States and East Africa. By the time I come back I will be able to tell you if it is also true of the Indians in Indonesia and Bali.

The Hindustan Times, 27 June 1987

Discovering the Assamese

'What is Assam? And where is Assam? These are some of the questions that often arise in inquisitive minds outside. It is more so in this period of our country's history and national reconstruction. To many outsiders, Assam is no more than a land of mountains and malaria, earthquakes and floods, and the Kamakhya temple.'

So writes Hem Barua in *The Red River & The Blue Hill*. My hotel room overlooks 'The Red River' except that at this time of the year, the Brahmaputra is a dull grey colour (it is said to turn red when in spate). The hills certainly look blue at a distance. Dominating the broad river and the twin cities of Guwahati and Dispur is the Nilachala hill with the temple of their patron goddess, Kamakhya. I had visited the temple on my first visit to Assam more than 20 years ago. By the *Debi's doya* (grace of the Goddess) I was allowed to come a third time to pay her my respects.

The temple of Kamakhya stands on Neel Parbat. As the legend goes, Lord Shiva was so overcome by mad frenzy when he heard of the death of his consort, Sati, that he carried her corpse over his shoulder round the world causing havoc everywhere. Ultimately, Lord Vishnu let loose his *Sudarshan Chakra* which cut up Sati's body into 51 pieces. Her genitals fell on Neel Parbat. The temple was originally built by Kamdev, the god of lust, who had been reduced to ashes by Lord Shiva for disturbing his meditation. He was forgiven and recreated in his original state. Hence the temple is named after him—Kamakhya or Kamrup. A sizeable township has gone up on the hill: There are the families of 15000 *pandas*, hostels for pilgrims, a high school, clinic and post office, a bazaar selling trinkets and flowers and hundreds of goats and baskets crammed with pigeons to be offered for sacrifice. Even on a non-auspicious day and hour when I went there, the queue of worshippers was over 200 yards long. Instead of taking my turn, which would have taken over an hour of queuing up, I went round the smaller shrines and ponds and then further uphill to the temple of Bhuwaneshwari Devi on the peak of Neel Parbat. There were only two college girls there to pray for success in their examinations. I sat on a rock outside the temple taking in the splendid panoramic view of the Brahmaputra, the mountains and the habitation below. The girls asked to be dropped off near the university. I asked them whether they were Assamese or Bengali—it is impossible to tell the difference. 'Assamese,' they replied in duet. 'You want to throw all outsiders out of Assam?' I asked them. They nodded their heads. 'All Bengalis, Marwaris, Punjabis, Biharis?' I asked again. Once again they nodded their heads. Later, my escort asked one of them her father's name and what he did. 'Hem Chandra Biswas,' she replied. 'He is in business.' Evidentally she was Bengali but preferred to call herself Assamese.

The Assamese have only themselves to blame for the massive inflow of outsiders. While they are rightly proud of having repelled repeated incursions of Mughal armies into the Brahmaputra valley, they remained blissfully unaware of the peace-loving Marwaris taking over most of their trade and commerce. Likewise Muslim peasantry from East Pakistan took possession of large parts of cultivable land. An Assamese proverb sums up the easy-going ways of the locals:

If the sun shines, he prefers the shade.
When in shade, he sleeps.
When the planting season is over, he plants
In a plot or two of land.

In the evening I went to take a look at the main shopping centre of Guwahati called Fancy Bazaar. Being Bihu time, it was crammed with shoppers buying gifts. Just about every shop was owned by Marwaris, Sindhis or Punjabis. Wholesale trading, in tea and vegetables, was entirely a Marwari monopoly. What riles the Assamese is not Marwari presence as much as their reluctance to invest their earnings in Assam, mix with the Assamese and make Assam their home. 'All that Assam has goes out of Assam—tea, petroleum, timber. Non-Assamese do exactly the same. Make their fortunes here to send back to their home states,' said a young Assamese to me. 'How long will the Assamese allow this state of affairs to go on?'

The Hindustan Times, 29 April 1989

■

Bhubaneshwar

Bhubaneshwar from *Bhawan* (abode) *Eeshwar* (God) or *Bhoomi* (earth) *Eeshwar,* has over 150 historic temples and tanks for worshippers to bathe in. The most frequented is the Lingaraj (the King of Lingas) temple of Lord Shiva alongside the large rectangular tank, Bindusagar (the Ocean of Semen). It was built in the 11th century and has some exquisite sculpture on its walls and a 48-metre-high tower. On holy days it is very difficult to enter it because of milling crowds. On any day it receives between 10,000 and 15,000 worshippers. As in other Hindu temples, the *pandas* never leave visitors alone. Their blessings are for sale; if you turn away, they curse you.

After the Lingaraj, the Mukteshwar temple appears like a haven of tranquillity. It has few worshippers but quite a few bathers. It has a natural spring whose waters are said to be endowed with powers of fertilizing barren women. On *Shivaratri,* the first few pails of water are sold for a thousand rupees per bucket. My favourite among Bhubaneshwar's temples is the Raja-Rani temple. It is not for worship and therefore free of crowds and *pandas*. It is modest sized and some of its sculpture as good as any other.

When it comes to sculpture you cannot match the Sun Temple at Konarak. Much of it is erotic in the minutest detail. But every slab of erotica is a masterpiece. It is the temples of Orissa, mostly Konarak, which provide the postures for Odissi dancers.

Seeing them in cold stone you wonder how young women manage to stick out their hips sideways and appear so enchantingly seductive. All you have to do is to watch a good Odissi dancer to see how it is done.

The Hindustan Times, 18 March 1989

■

Dateline Dhaka

Dhaka is vast open spaces with well laid-out parks and gardens. Also, bazaars more crammed with humanity than Calcutta's slums. And more bicycle rickshaws than any other city in the world. Government offices are in modern buildings surrounded by lawns; trading and commerce is done in crabby little shops and kiosks. The prime minister's secretariat still smells of fresh paint and concrete. His hall-sized room has only one picture, that of President General Husain Muhammed Ershad. Besides his working table, there are a sofa and two armchairs for visitors.

'What would you like to see in Bangladesh?' he asks me. I reply with a counter-question. 'What would you like me to see in Bangladesh?'

After a long pause he suggests, 'Perhaps something you have not seen before. Our up-Zila self-governing schemes. We give money to a group of villages, and let them decide how to spend it: on roads, health, education, or whatever. They are the elected bodies—

democracy at the grass roots. The local MP is also involved in these decisions and has to spend quite a bit of his time in his constituency. Then we have a new drug policy. We've banned import of all except life-saving drugs. It's given our pharmaceutical industry a big boost.'

I chip in. 'We in India would like to know what Islamicization of Bangladesh means to the non-Muslims; your views about problems with India—distribution of river waters, flood control, boundary disputes, control of the ocean bed etc. For the rest, just let me loiter around and get a feel of the place.'

He made a note of my requests and fixed appointments for me.

I started with loitering around. I went to the most popular *dargah* of the city. The tomb of Hazrat Khwaja Sharfuddin Chisti of Baghdad, who brought Islam to Bangladesh in the 14th century is in the compound of the High Court. Since it was mid-morning, there were more beggars than worshippers. Worship of holy men and their tombs, forbidden by Islam, has in fact become the pillar of Islam in Eastern countries where idol worship is the common thing. It also struck me as odd that despite the wave of fundamentalism sweeping Muslim countries, I didn't come across a single Bangladeshi woman wearing a *burkha*. Most Muslim women wore *bindis* on their foreheads and a few even *sindoor* in the parting of their hair just as Hindu women.

*

New Year's eve is a great event for the elite of Dhaka. All five star hotels and clubs are fully booked. The *crème de la crème* of Dhaka society and once the Whites, and now the Brown Sahibs' exclusive preserve is the Dacca Club. 'You must see the New Year in at the Dacca Club,' said everyone I met. I did not realize there might be a design behind exposing me to it.

We arrived at 9 p.m. to be received by the President, and were shown to the high table close to the stage. The football field-sized lawn had been covered over by a canvas roof to make a dining room, to accommodate over 2000 guests at separate tables. Multicoloured lights everywhere. The music was so loud that you had to shout at the top of your voice to be heard. I was introduced to two young men. One I gathered later was professor of economics from Toronto University, nominated finance minister of Bangladesh. The other, a boyish-looking product of Oxford, was Bangladesh Ambassador to Peking. A bottle of Johnnie Walker Black Label was placed before us. By the time one round had been served, it was empty and promptly replaced by another. Ladies sitting alongside had bottles of fizzy Cokes and 7 Ups. The gentleman at my left and one facing him exchanged cigars—Havanas each costing over 600 takas (Rs 300). We had barely been introduced when the master of ceremonies announced that the floor was ready for dancing. Ear piercing rock-n-roll music put an end to all conversation. The dance floor was soon packed with gyrating men and women. This modern dance involves no body contact and yet produces all the movements of copulation. I watched and drank. In the hour and a half I was there, four more bottles of Scotch were emptied at our table. There was no sign of dinner. 'Not before 11 p.m.,' said the waiter. We took our leave. Outside, chauffeurs and policemen were swilling beer and exchanging pleasantries. Whatever else Islamization may entail, it fights a losing battle against good living.

At Hotel Sonargaon, the scene was much the same as it had been at the club. Crowds drinking (beer rather than Scotch) and dancing. We were in bed by the time crackers exploded to announce the birth of 1989. So what does declaration of Islam as State religion amount to? Will Bangladesh introduce Shariat law? 'Certainly not,' said everyone I questioned. 'Purdah for women?' 'Never,' came the unanimous verdict. 'Prohibition of liquor?' 'You must be joking!' they replied, raising their glasses.

The Hindustan Times, 21 January 1989

■

The French connection

Much has been written on the 200th anniversary celebrations of the French Revolution and its influence on Western thinking. It had no immediate impact on Asia. For one, what was happening in Paris came to be known in these parts many months later. What would our great great grandsires have made of the storming of the Bastille or the guillotining of Louis XVI, Marie Antoinette and thousands of well-to-do citizens? Concepts like equality, liberty and fraternity must have sounded very odd to people steeped in monarchic and feudal traditions. The only Indian who seemed to have responded to the call from France was Tipu Sultan of Mysore who assumed the title *Citoyen Tipu*. This was more to ingratiate himself with his French allies in his wars against the English than acquiescing to notions of freedom or equality.

French presence in India was of too short a duration to leave any permanent impression on Indian thinking or way of living. Although hundreds of French soldiers of fortune rose to high positions in the armies of the Marathas and the Sikhs, they did not stay with their employers long enough to be able to Frenchify them. They introduced French words of command in the army, French wines, brandy, champagne and perfumes to the courts of the Indian aristocracy, but hardly any Indians outside their dwindling possessions learnt their language or read their literature in translation.

It was after the First World War that Indians began to discover France. And that, largely because Indian students studying in British universities found the atmosphere in France comparatively freer of racial prejudice, living much cheaper, the food and wine more appetizing and French women more attractive and forthcoming than those they encountered in England. When I first went to Paris in the 1930s, there were barely a handful of Indians living there and not a single Indian restaurant. A Sikh was still a strange sight. For some reason, street urchins, when they spotted me, shouted, 'Ali Baba!' Young ladies asked me to read their palms. Most thought that I wore a turban because I was a magician.

I picked up a certain amount of French from Berlitz and summer courses on French literature organized by Sorbonne University. The French have this pig-headed snobbishness about their language. They refuse to learn any other and do not really open up with anyone who does not speak French. I found the going much easier after I was able to converse with them. I spent all my holidays in France: in winter, skiing in the French Alps; in summer, doing the tennis circuit in Brittany, sea-bathing and flirting on the Cote d'Azur at Nice or Cannes. It was always more rewarding than holidaying in England or in other countries of Europe. France was less inhibited: you could see beautiful naked girls dance in Folies Bergiere; you could go to night clubs catering to all kinds of sexual deviants; you could read books banned in England and America; you could kill yourself with drink or drugs. Nobody objected.

Things changed rapidly after the Second World War. France became more expensive to live in than England. And less tolerant towards coloured people because of the troubles they were having hanging on to their African colonies. The two years I spent with UNESCO in Paris proved financially disastrous for me. Despite the high, tax-free salary and diplomatic privileges, I was out of pocket by several thousand dollars. The one thing I found more irritating than their unfriendliness was their obsession with money. The French are more money-minded than any other people I have met. And more demanding of *baksheesh* than Indian beggars. They are the originators of 'service charge' after you have paid for the service you got, and have an ever-extended palm for *pourboire*—tips. The usherette who flashes her torch in the cinema to show you your seat expects a tip, the boy who shows you the boat you have hired and paid for wants a tip; so do cab-drivers, waiters and chamber maids. A foreigner can go crazy working out how much to give for these non-services.

However, I discovered why Paris had become the favourite city for émigré writers, poets, painters and dancers. In no other country in the world is a creative artist given more respect than in France. I wrote two novels in France. One over weekends in a bistro named *Saint Jean au Bois* deep in the forest of Compiegne; the other in a cottage I had rented in Faviers village near Houdan, about 60 kilometres south of Paris. In both places, the villagers treated me with deference as *Monsieur Le Ecrivain*—the writer.

Sunday, 26 August 1989

Nagaland on Christmas eve

In Kohima, the day dawns an hour and a half earlier
than in Delhi. By 5.30 a.m. the sky is bright, etching
deckle-edged mountain peaks. Life also begins earlier.
Naga men and women wrapped in their colourful
shawls saunter down the hills towards the town centre.
Women squat by the roadside and empty out sacks of
tomatoes, potatoes, onions and garlic they have
brought from their farmsteads. Roadsides become
vegetable markets.

I make my courtesy call on Chief Minister S.C. Jamir.
His wife serves us coffee. He briefs me on his problems
without saying a word about politics. Development
projects? They are a long distance from Kohima. As
far as I am concerned he would be happy if I simply
write about the beauteous landscape, its flora and
fauna. I am happy to do that because I don't have to
exaggerate. It is a beautiful mountainous country with
a very friendly, ever-smiling people. Kohima could offer
everything that Darjeeling, Dalhousie, Shimla or
Mussoorie have—and more fresh air and less
congestion. Only silly government rules which forbid
foreigners from entering and the requirement of permits
for others inhibit flow of tourist traffic. Naga insurgency
which explains the ubiquitous presence of the Indian
army is all but dead. Indian Nagas have made peace
with India. It will take the over-cautious babus of New
Delhi who find it safer to say 'not yet' quite a lot of
pressure to give the green signal for Nagaland to be

opened up. As it is, the Japfu Ashoka, Kohima's best appointed hotel, gaily done up for Christmas, has only two guests—my wife and I. That's what a slow-moving, dim-witted bureaucracy can do to hamper prosperity.

Nagaland has enormous tourist potential. At the moment they are concentrating on Kohima and Dimapur. New tourist lodges are to be built in the capital; artificial lakes and a water front at Dimapur. From Kohima, treks will be organized to Mount Japfu and two picturesque valleys, Dzukou and Dzulake. Dimapur will also have its own wildlife sanctuary at Intangki, close to Assam's Kaziranga. A lake has already come up at Shiloi, where a hydroelectric project is in the making. Kohima may soon offer a cheaper, better, and more accessible alternative (as a summer hill resort) to Darjeeling to people who long to escape from the sweltering heat of Bengal to breathe fresh, cool mountain air.

The Kohima zoo is a bare five minutes' drive from the CM's residence. I am not much of a zoo-goer but am determined to see species I have not seen before. In Papua New Guinea, I travelled 50 miles to see the Bird of Paradise. In Indonesia, I trudged all morning round its enormous zoological gardens to see the man-eating, crocodile-sized lizard, the Komodo Dragon. In Kohima, my quest was the pheasant famed for its beauteous colouring, the Blythe's Tragopan, now almost extinct in its natural habitat. It turned out to be a hazardous pilgrimage. The zoo is built along a steep hillside and I had to climb up over 500 steps to get to the aviary. However, the higher I got, the more rewarding was the bird's-eye-view of Kohima. My spirits were dampened by the thought that I'd have to go down the same steps. With my bifocals, going down has become quite a risk. At my age, one fall and a broken bone would mean the end of my active life. However, I did get to see the Tragopan. It is indeed a thing of beauty—golden red frontage and a deep blue body flecked with white diamonds. Like other pheasants, it is obviously a table delicacy. The morning paper recorded the killing of 200 of these protected birds in some sanctuary. The Kohima zoo is meant to be a breeding centre. There were barely a dozen birds there. Apparently some had managed to escape. They are now being bred in England by the World Wildlife Fund.

The Hindustan Times, 17 February 1990

■

The heart of India

Where is real India to be found? Certainly not in the metropolitan cities like Calcutta, Bombay or Madras— all three creations of the British. Nor alas any longer in Delhi where all that was worthwhile in the culture of Shahjahanabad has been swamped under the deluge of Punjabis, *sarkari babus* and the diplomatic corps. After considering the pros and cons of the cities that remain, I have decided to vote for Hyderabad as the heart of India.

Why?

For one, Hyderabad is in the centre of India. It is also on the line of the great ethnic-linguistic divide between the Aryan Hindi-speaking north and the Dravidian Telugu-, Kannada-, Tamil-, Malayali-speaking south. In Hyderabad you will meet many people who can speak half-a-dozen Indian languages with equal fluency. This cannot be said of any of our other cities.

For another, Hyderabad has more of the Hindu-Muslim melange of people, cultures and ways of living than other cities. This is understandable as the two communities are almost even in numbers and the Deccan has always been the meeting point and the melting pot of southern and northern ways of living. Here, along the same street you will find restaurants serving *idli, sambar, dosa* as well as *biryani, burra kababs* and *haleem*. In the same hall on alternate evenings you can attend *kavi sammelans* and *mushairas*, listen to *qawwalis* and *kirtans*, watch Bharatnatyam and Kathak. Can you get all these with the same facility in any other Indian city?

In the days gone by, Hyderabad had a lot more to say for itself which it can say no more. It had its own unique brand of aristocracy of the world's most beautiful people with gracious speech and manners and an expensive way of life. Their palaces and mansions have been converted into schools, colleges, circuit-houses and government offices. Its famous Salar Jang collection (it never deserved the title of a museum) is today rightly described as Salar junk because it is no more than an assortment of bric-a-brac which gives more evidence of the Nawab Sahib's greed for acquiring things, than of his aesthetic taste. The once-colourful red light district, *Mehboob-ki-Mehndi* has been 'cleansed' of all its *mehboobas*. Its salubrious Banjara Hill has been blasted to near extinction. A city designed to accommodate 1,00,000, now shelters over two million people.

Nevertheless, a lot remains. And a lot more could be done to make Hyderabad India's most attractive city. Apart from three summer months—April, May and June—it has a very pleasant climate. And nowhere have I experienced a more exhilarating monsoon than in Hyderabad. A fresh breeze blows all the time; the skies are a kaleidoscope of changing patterns varying from nimbus black and snow-white mountains to a scatter of partridge feathers. Even when the skies are clear and the sun shines brightly, it seldom becomes oppressive as strong winds pick up waters from the innumerable lakes in the vicinity and cool the city like *khas*-screened air coolers.

The Parliament has often toyed with the idea of holding some of its sessions in the south. I am sure if it held one monsoon session in Hyderabad, no MPs would want to return to Delhi.

The Hindustan Times, August 1983

Speaking of Sex

Kama to Rama

There are many ways of attaining godhood, say teachers of religion. Acharya Rajneesh disagrees and says there is only one way and sexual intercourse is the first step towards it. He maintains that religion as it is practised is false, and its propagators are agents of Satan. They have degraded love and taught us the negation of life. The philosophy of religion has always been death-oriented instead of being life-oriented. He goes on to add: 'I call religion the art of living. Religion is not a way to undermine life; it is a medium for delving deeply into the mysteries of existence. Religion is not turning one's back on life; it is facing life squarely. Religion is not escaping from life; religion is embracing life fully. Religion is the total realization of life.'

Since love is the essence of all religions and sex the essence of love, you cannot sidestep it to proceed on your voyage of discovery. Rajneesh writes, 'Sex is the beginning of the journey to love. The origin, the Gangotri of the Ganges of Love, is sex, passion—and everybody behaves like its enemy. Every culture, every religion, every guru, every seer has attacked this Gangotri, this source, and the river has remained bottled up. The hue and cry has always been, "Sex is sin. Sex is irreligious. Sex is poison." But we never seem to realize that ultimately, it is the sex energy itself that travels to and reaches the inner ocean of love. Love is the transformation of sex energy.'

Because sex has been condemned and suppressed, 'it has become an obsession, a disease, a perversion', says the Acharya, and advises us to 'accept sex with joy. Acknowledge its sacredness . . . When a man approaches his wife he should have a sacred feeling, as if he were going to a temple. And when a wife goes to her husband she should be full of the reverence one has nearing God. In the moments of sex, lovers pass through coitus, and that stage is very near to the temple of God, to where he is manifest in creative formlessness.' He conjectures that man had his first glimpse of *samadhi* during sexual intercourse culminating in a climax when the mind becomes empty of thoughts. Thus *vishyanand* (bliss of coitus) and *Brahmanand* (bliss of union with God) are much the same; one is ephemeral, the other eternal.

Not all sexual intercourse is experience of divinity. For that you have to first get rid of your ego—'Unless I dissolve myself, how can the other unite with me?' he asks. Love always gives; the ego is ever the grabber; love is motiveless, the ego always motivated; the ego only understands the language of taking; the language of giving is love. The second condition to be fulfilled is the feeling of timelessness. 'In orgasm, the sense of time is non-existent. There is no past, no future, there is only the present moment.'

The Acharya has some practical suggestions to overcome an unhealthy obsession with sexuality. Children should be allowed to remain nude as much as possible in the home so that they do not develop prurient curiosity in private organs. They should also be taught to meditate (on what, he does not say) in silence for at least one hour every day. They should be taught what sex is all about before they are old enough to engage in it. He writes, 'Sex is the most mysterious, most profound, most precious and, at the same time, the most accursed subject; and we are in total darkness about it. We never pay our attention to this important phenomenon. A man goes through the routine of coitus throughout his life, but he does not know what it is.'

The Acharya, who claims to have had sexual fulfilment in his previous life which cleared his mind of sexuality for his present incarnation and those to come, tells us how to get the best out of coitus. Most of us are used to quickies which end in frustration and incite us to have more of the same thing. Coitus, he tells us, must be prolonged as much as possible. In the way of techniques, he suggests slowing down one's breathing and focusing awareness to a point between the eyes, the seat of the *agnichakra*. If you can prolong intercourse to one hour, you need not think of sex for the rest of your life; if you can prolong to three hours, you will be liberated from sexuality for your lives to come. A third essential condition is that you should approach sex with reverence. 'Give sex a sacred status in your life,' he says. 'At the time of coitus, we are close to God.'

The Acharya tells us the sculptors of erotica on the temples of Konark, Khajuraho and Puri had the right approach to sex. We should have such temples all over

India. *Tantriks* were also on the right path; preachers of religious dogma suppressed them. He concludes: 'The journey to *kama* is also the journey to Rama. The journey to lust is also the journey to light. The tremendous attraction for sex is also the search for the sublime.'

It is difficult to decide how seriously one can take Rajneesh. As anything else he writes, his *From Sex to Super-Consciousness* is extremely readable.

Sunday, 12 August 1989

■

Hand of the Potter

I have in hand what must be India's first journal for homosexuals—gays and lesbians. Vol. I No. 1 of *Bombay Dost* has 18 pages, half in English, half in Hindi, and is priced at Rs 5. It is for private circulation only and gives neither the name of the editor-cum-publisher nor its address. I expect this is to save itself from being harassed by the police.

Personally I have absolutely nothing against homosexuality as I regard it as natural as bi-sexuality. Some people are born that way; it also exists in the animal world. Omar Khayyam was right in his judgement on the Divine Potter who moulded us from lumps of clay:

One answered this, but after silence spake
A vessel of a more ungainly make;
'They sneer at me for leaning all awry;
What! did the hand then of the
Potter shake?'

You will have noticed that homosexuals often have ungainly shapes and their exaggerated gestures betray their sexual inclinations.

There is a lot of confusion in the minds of people over the division of sexes. Most regard the line dividing males from females as sharp and clear: the incidence of hermaphroditism as an aberration of nature, effeminacy in men and masculinity in women as unnatural deviations. None of these assumptions are correct. As a matter of fact, there is no such clear black and white divide between the sexes as males and females have masculine and feminine characteristics of different proportions in them; there is something of the woman in every man and something of the man in every woman. These traits surface at different times and in different circumstances in their lives. Hardly anyone goes through life without some homosexual experience or the other. Boys are exposed to it at school and college. Girls have crushes on their teachers or on each other during their adolescence. In purely male or female institutions like jails, ashrams, convents, monasteries and the army, homosexuality is rampant. The vast majority of men and women grow out of it. A small minority continue to have homosexual or lesbian relationships because they find them more emotionally fulfilling. For some reason their incidence is higher amongst sensitive, creative people like artists, musicians, dancers, etc. than the ordinary run of humanity. These liaisons can be intensely marked with violent jealousies and may be life-long. What confuses the sexual scene further is the fact that many of them are heterosexual. Thus we have people like Oscar Wilde who was for a time a devoted husband and father as well as a pederast. We had our own Amrita Shergil who had numerous affairs with men as well as women, and died as a married woman. We also had the celebrated nuclear physicist, Dr Homi Bhaba, who, like many homosexuals, had a life-long attachment to an elderly female. Also the eminent writer, Aubrey Menen, who had a permanent male lover, continued to solicit other men till the last days of his life. I know many celebrities of today who are likewise 'ambidextrous'; for obvious reasons I cannot name them. I have both respect and admiration for some of them.

Do homosexuals need to have a journal of their own? *Bombay Dost* goes beyond being a forum of affirmation of homosexuality. It provides information about where you can find others similarly inclined. In Bombay, you may meet them in the evening at the Gateway of India. In Delhi, at the new Coffee Home. Signals for recognition are provided by the colour of shirts you may wear, or by a rose placed on the table where you may sit with others of the ilk. In the West they wear one earring in the right ear. I find this a somewhat crude form of soliciting. I have also personal objection to the Hindi word for 'gay'. It is *khush,* and the fraternity described as *khushdosts.* I repeat that although I have absolutely nothing against them, I wish homosexuals would choose a name which bears no resemblance to mine: I am not one of them.

Sunday, 30 June 1990

■

Living longer: Making love to the last

There are no clearly-defined borders between youth, middle and old age. Some young men and women become middle-aged in their thirties, others remain young in their fifties and sixties; some become impotent in their youth; others continue to enjoy sex into their eighties. Indeed, most people will agree that as long as you are capable of enjoying sex, you are young; when the sexual urge disappears, you have become old. Men are more obsessed with proving their potency than women and, when natural impulses begin to wane, will try all kinds of aphrodisiacs to keep going. Unfortunately for them, so far, medical science has not produced any reliable sex rejuvenants. Good health and worldly success are more potent than any *kushta.* Henry Kissinger was hundred per cent right when he said that power is the ultimate aphrodisiac. So we find so many successful politicians compulsive womanizers. Equally potent is the company of the young and the vivacious.

Sexual urges are generated by hormones secreted by the pituitary gland located beneath the brain, the testes, and in the case of women, in the ovaries. These age with the ageing of their owners. Also, in monogamous marriages, the absence of variety (which is indeed the spice of life when it comes to sex) and monotony deprive both partners of the urge to engage in lovemaking. Statistics show that in marriages which have lasted more than twenty years, the sex urge has all but disappeared. Attempts to revive it with the same partner are not successful, but failure to do so does not impair matrimonial closeness. Men in their fifties and sixties are still capable of sex once a week. The urge tapers off in the seventies and is usually extinct in the eighties.

But both men and women hanker after sex even after the natural urge has abated. The natural way to prolong the sex urge are liaisons with younger people. Ageing men are drawn towards girls younger than their daughters and young girls respond to overtures of men who become their father figures. Likewise, older women take on young lovers who see in them their mother-mistresses. The relationships are utterly Freudian, utterly unnatural, but utterly fulfilling for both partners even if the sex in the relationships is not satisfactory.

One sure way to impotence is to ignore the presence of attractive members of the opposite sex. Men and women who take to religion in their later lives and spend most of their time in the company of their own age group age prematurely and lose the zest for living.

For those anxious to revive their sex lives, there are hormone injections which revive potency for fifteen days. Most pathetic are cases of men who have the desire but are unable to perform. Even for them medical science has found stuff to inject into their genitals to revive them. Experiments are afoot to produce a pill which will have the same effect.

Heavy drinking over many years can have disastrous effects on male or female potency. Alcohol may temporarily whip up desire, but it robs the drinker of the power to perform. Fortunately, most drinking men in their late seventies and eighties if given the choice between a willing female and a slug of premium Scotch, will opt for the latter.

The Hindustan Times, 10 February 1996

The Way We Are

The Chaudhry Obsession

It starts by being a complex and then turns into an obsession. As a complex it manifests itself in the form of a compulsive desire to be a Mr Somebody in every situation—a member of every committee—if already a member, then its treasurer, secretary, vice-president or president. To be the centre of attention at every party, the bridegroom at every wedding, the corpse at every funeral. If the desire is not firmly curbed when it raises its head, it soon turns into an obsession. You can see it in epidemic form in India. Every villager wants to become a *sarpanch,* every social worker a politician, every politician an MLA or MP, and every MP a Cabinet minister or the prime minister. There is no other explanation of the phenomenon of thousands of aspirants at every election—over 300 in one constituency.

The Chaudhry Complex manifests itself fairly early in life and assumes menacing proportions by campus-age. You must have known boys who were forever wanting to be elected to something or the other: member of the canteen committee, carom club executive, university union or whatever. Thereafter the same kind of fellows want to be somebodies in their *beopar mandals,* FICCIs, Rotary Clubs, Lions Clubs, or whatever. They append catalogues of what they succeeded in becoming on their visiting cards and letterheads of their stationery. I knew a buffoon whose writing pads had his entire biodata printed in the margin. He was the greatest clown in college because he wanted to be captain of every team. Later he became a minister, Governor and an ambassador. Then there are fellows who append honorary doctorates conferred on them as if they were men of medicine or learning. The same applies to government honours. There are regulations to the effect that they must not be used as honorifics. They are. See the number of chaps who describe themselves as Padma Shri or Padma Bhushan so and so.

The most ludicrous examples of the Chaudhry obsession can be seen at club elections: the more elite the institution, the more blatant the exercise in one-upmanship. In the recent elections of the Delhi Gymkhana Club, members were bombarded with letters soliciting votes. Without exception all of them extolled the status of the aspirant: IFS, IAS, IPS, Squadron Leader, and more insidious than these in a club half of whose membership comprises businessmen, chartered accountants, lawyers with taxation problems, were arm-twisting appendages like Indian Revenue Service or Commissioner of income tax. Believe it or not, these descriptions were even printed on the ballot paper.

What do these jokers get by becoming Chaudhrys? Not money (though some wouldn't mind making a little on the side) but patronage. And for a time, being *jee huzoored* by the staff. Little things affect little minds as small pants fit small behinds.

Sunday, 6 April 1985

A Nation of Sycophants

Are we Indians more prone to sycophancy than other people? I think we are but I have never been able to fathom why it is so pervasive. Everyone of any consequence has his or her coterie of *chamchas*. The *chamchas* explain their attachment to their heroes as devotion or loyalty. So in any organization we have a pecking order.

The top person is treated like a *devta* (deity) or *anndata* (provider). He has a small circle of *chamchas* who will do anything at his bidding, suffer being treated like doormats, snubbed and humiliated in public, but never waiver in their single-minded devotion to their boss: they will serve him, his family, cultivate his friends, hate his enemies and do their utmost to identify themselves with the person they adore.

Though sycophancy flourishes in all societies, it has deeper, emotional and spiritual roots in India. Dr Bhimrao Ambedkar, the chief drafter of our Constitution, made a perceptive analysis of sycophancy in Indian life in a speech in the Constituent Assembly. He said:

'For in India, Bhakti or what may be called the path of devotion or hero-worship, plays a part in its politics unequalled in magnitude by the part it plays in the politics of any other country in the world. Bhakti in religion may be a road to the salvation of the soul. But in politics, Bhakti or hero-worship is a sure road to degradation and to eventual dictatorship. Bhakti has certainly led to unjust attitudes towards a leader other than the current hero.'

I think Dr Ambedkar was right. It was the general acceptance of Bhakti as the best path to salvation throughout India with corresponding acceptance of Islamic Sufism which likewise emphasized the need of total surrender to the spiritual guide which turned into sycophancy in secular life. The Guru or the Murshid who required dedication of *tan, man, dhan*—body, mind and wordly wealth—the *chelas* gave it to them in pursuit of spiritual salvation. Today they give it to their bosses with the same spirit of dedication to attain wordly success.

The Tribune, 8 June 1996

■

Problems of Old Age

You have to be old to know what the real problems of ageing are. As an old English proverb goes: 'Only the toad beneath the harrow knows where each point of the harrow goes.'

I am not talking of physical or mental infirmities which come with the years and need special medical treatment. Nor of the indifference of sons, daughters and grandchildren who find their grandparents' growing senility and anecdotage a nuisance and would like them to depart from the world to make life easier for them.

I am not even talking of the shortage of old people's homes where the aged could spend their last days in reasonable comfort and die in peace. What I am talking about is the callous indifference and lack of consideration of the common people towards those who can no longer keep pace with them. Let me give you a few examples from personal life.

For many years we spent at least one evening of the week with our friend of over 60 years, Prem Kirpal. He lived less than 50 yards from us across the road. Till some years ago we used to simply walk over taking the road divider in our strides. Then the divider became a hurdle: stepping on it became as hard a feat as scaling Everest; stepping down from it on the other side became even more hazardous. We circumvented the hurdle and found a break in the road divider. The next problem was to wait for a suitable gap in the speeding traffic to get to the middle of the road and wait for a similar break in the stream of cars, buses and scooters coming from the other direction and hobble across as fast as our legs could carry us. I am reminded of the Urdu couplet:

Javaani jaatee rahee
Aur hamein pataa bhee na laga;
Isee ko dhoond rahey hain
Kamar jhukaae hooey
(Youth faded away
And we did not as much as

notice it going.)

We are up against another problem, more serious than dining with a friend. In the summer months we used to go to Kasauli two or three times. I used to drive all the way. Then the traffic on the Grand Trunk Road and the 22 miles from Kalka to Kasauli became too heavy for comfort.

We took to going by train: the Himalayan Queen to Chandigarh, then by car to Kasauli. Then we had to give up the Himalayan Queen for the simple reason that this train left from and came to different platforms of New Delhi Railway station which entailed going up and down steps of overbridges.

We could not negotiate coming down because of the danger of being knocked down by people running down in a hurry. Now, even though as an ex-MP I could travel free, we go by the Shatabdi Express and pay Rs 1,300 each way for the simple reason that the train leaves and arrives on Platform Number One and there are no overbridges to cross. Even so, boarding and getting off trains has become a nightmarish experience. Stations and platforms are crowded. Everyone seems to be in a desperate hurry to get in or get off the train. The *dhakkam dhakka* (shoving and pushing) can knock down old people and fracture their brittle bones. Travelling by air is only marginally easier. I have to request the staff or some able-bodied fellow-passengers to help me with hand baggage. I realize my days of travel are fast coming to a close.

What are old people to do? *Vanaprastha*—retirement to the jungles—is the prescription suggested by our sacred texts. I am beginning to come to the conclusion that they had the right answer.

The Tribune, 19 July 1997

■

Yuppies, The Future of India

Until a few months ago, I wasn't aware of the existence of yuppies. They have been around for almost 30 years and are said to be almost extinct. Now I see references to them in many journals. I could not find them in any of my dictionaries.

'Yuppy' is an elongation of YUP, an acronym for 'young urban professional'. Another variation was 'yumpy', for 'upwardly mobile professional'. They are to be distinguished from yippies, a group of brash iconoclasts who nominated a pig as President of the United States in 1968, as also from Flower Children, the progeny of affluent parents who advocated freedom to do anything anyone wanted. Yuppies, of whose existence I learnt after their demise, consisted of young (under 50) people coming from wealthy backgrounds with degrees from well-known universities and making a lot of money on their own: the minimum earning for qualifying as a yuppy was 35,000 dollars per year. At one time they were also known as baby boomers because lots of them were born after World War II. The elite amongst the yuppies were dinks (double income no kids) where both husband and wife had handsome incomes and had decided not to have children. At one time they had become a dominant political and cultural force in American society.

Although yuppies did not form a distinctly identifiable group, this freemasonry of the young-rich evolved a recognizable lifestyle: a BMW sports car, penthouse with a large pedigreed dog like a Saint Bernard or an Afghan hound and the best of clothes—shirts from Brooks Brothers and ties from Van Heusen. They cultivated sophistication in apprehension of art, music and literature, ignored politicians and upstarts, ate frugal salad-based meals and rarely went to church.

As often happens, what was fashionable in America becomes the rage in India some years later: the Indian yuppy is coming into his own. My acquaintance with the Bharati young-rich is limited to breeds spawned in northern India, mainly with Punjabi or Marwari pedigrees. Let me point to some features which may help you to identify him. Like the American, the Indian yuppy is the son of a wealthy father and is not a nouveau riche. But unlike his American counterpart of yesteryear, he is not the product of a renowned public school or institute of higher learning like the Jawaharlal Nehru University or one of the IITs: their products end up as civil servants or box*walas*. Our Yuppy has a degree in commerce from a second-rate college, is familiar with American business terminology which he pronounces with an imitated nasal twang and mispronounces most other English words. He often lives with his parents but maintains a separate kitchen. He owns an air-conditioned Mercedes, Toyota or Datsun. He wears gold or platinum rings with lucky stones, and occasionally, a charm round his neck. He has the most expensive Swiss-made gold watch—Cartier, Omega, Rolex or a custom-made Patek Phillipe bearing his initials—and wears it facing inwards. He buys Hindi comics and film magazines like *Stardust, Filmfare* or *Cine Blitz* at airports and travels executive class. Once a fortnight he takes his wife and children to a Hindi movie. He drinks premium brand Scotch in five-star hotels. He calls on his guru at some ashram once a month, and when out of his hometown, has *bandobast* with a call-girl. He is the future hope of India.

Sunday, 6 June 1987

■

Mama's Darlings

Some days ago I received at letter from a Dutch girl. It was unusually candid about her personal life. She had been in love with an Indian boy. They had lived together for two years and planned to get married. Without warning, the Indian walked out and tamely married one of his own relatives chosen for him by his mother. I have known innumerable young Indian men in love who, when it comes to marriage, let down their girlfriends on the plea *'Mummy nahin maantee.'* In this matter, our girls show more guts: if their parents don't agree, they simply run off with men they have given their hearts to. And still stranger, though we are often told that an Indian male is Papa-dominated and cannot make his own decisions till his father is dead (Koestler described Indian society as a 'Bapucracy'), when it comes to choosing a wife, it is the mother more than the father who imposes her wishes on her son.

How this Mama-domination has come about in a male-dominated society has been lucidly explained by the eminent psychiatrist Sudhir Kakar in a psycho-analytic study of childhood and society in India in his eminently readable book, *The Inner World.* Kakar is of the opinion that although an Indian girl is regarded as someone's daughter, wife or mother, her lower status builds strong ties between her and her son which the son finds hard to break. In her parents' home she is only a sojourner marking time to depart when she is given away in marriage. In her husband's house she is like a newly-acquired slave carrying out the wishes of her mother-in-law, husband's sisters and his elder brother's wives—in short, she is less a wife and more a daughter-in-law. A spectacular change in her status takes place when she becomes pregnant. Writes Kakar: 'It is only with motherhood that she comes into her own as a woman, and can make a place for herself in the family, in the community and in the life cycle. This accounts for her unique sense of maternal obligation and her readiness for practically unlimited emotional investment in her children.'

Indian mothers fuss over their sons much more than women of other countries fuss over theirs. Some continue to breast-feed them till they are five, caress and cuddle them as women caress and cuddle their lovers. This generates the notion in the male child: 'I am lovable, for I am loved.' Kakar infers: 'Many character traits ascribed to Indians are a part of the legacy of this particular pattern of infancy: trusting friendliness with a quick readiness to form attachments, and intense, if short-lived, disappointment if friendly overtures are not reciprocated; willingness to reveal the most intimate aspects about one's life at the slightest acquaintance and the expectation of a reciprocal familiarity in others.' It is this 'emotional capital built up during infancy', as Kakar describes it, that makes the Indian male his 'Mama's boy' for the rest of his life and incapable of giving his girlfriend or wife the love they expect from him.

Kakar cites many instances of the close mother-son relationship. Of his mother Nehru wrote: 'I had no fear of her, for I knew that she would condone everything I did and because of her excessive and undiscriminating love for me, I tried to dominate over her a little.' More forthright was Swami Yoganand: 'Father was kind, grave, at times stern. Loving him dearly, we children yet observed a certain reverential distance. But mother was Queen of hearts, and taught us only through love.'

Question: 'Why do Indian men make such lousy lovers?'

Answer: 'They get all the love they want from their mothers and by the time they attain puberty they become emotionally impotent.'

Sunday, 30 August 1986

Stray Thoughts

Tagore's National Anthem

Now that I have thrust my hand in the hornets' nest by criticizing Tagore's fiction, I may as well take up another contentious issue: the genesis of his song *Jana Gana Mana* which we adopted as our national anthem. At the recent BJP convention, proceedings began with the singing of *Vande Mataram* instead of *Jana Gana Mana*.

It is possible that Messrs Advani and Murli Manohar Joshi harbour the suspicion that *Jana Gana Mana* was composed in honour of King George V's visit to India. Tagore denied it but the suspicion that it was so started from the day it was first sung in public. This happened at the All India Congress Conference in 1911 at Calcutta. The session began on 26 December with the singing of *Vande Mataram*. The next day (27 December) was devoted to speeches welcoming King George.

It was on this day that *Jana Gana Mana* was sung. The session ended with the singing of Rajbhuja Dutt Choudhary's *Badshah Hamara*. Many Calcutta papers assumed that Tagore's song was also in the same vein. *The Statesman* of 28 December 1911 wrote: 'The Bengali poet Babu Rabindranath Tagore sang a song composed by him specially to welcome the Emperor.' *The Englishman* of the same date wrote: 'The proceedings began with the singing by Babu Rabindranath Tagore of a song specially composed by him in honour of the Emperor.'

The Indian of 29 December accepted the version: 'When the proceedings of the Indian National Congress began on Wednesday December 27, 1911, a Bengali song in welcome of the Emperor was sung. A resolution welcoming the Emperor and Empress was also adopted unanimously.'

If Tagore did not agree with this interpretation of his composition, he certainly said nothing about it at the time. It is more than likely that Indians then did not make any distinction between loyalty to the country and loyalty to the King Emperor. Besides that, Bengalis had good reason to be grateful to King George: he formally annulled the partition of Bengal made by Lord Curzon in 1905 which was bitterly resented by Bengali Hindus.

It was much later that Tagore himself categorically asserted that the words '*Bharat Bhagya Vidhata*' did not refer to the King or the Prince of Wales but to God. We must accept the Gurudev's word.

When the question of choosing a national anthem for the country came up before the Constituent Assembly, the choice was between *Vande Mataram* and *Jana Gana Mana*. Iqbal's *Saarey Jahaan Se Achha Hindustan Hamara* was put out of reckoning because Iqbal had been recognized as one of the founder-fathers of Pakistan. Gandhiji was in favour of *Vande Mataram*.

On 29 August 1947, he said *Vande Mataram* should be set to music so that millions can sing it together and feel the thrill. They should all sing in the same raga, with the same *bhava*. Shantiniketan or some other competent institution should design an acceptable raga.

What settled the issue in favour of *Jana Gana Mana* was the strong Bengali lobby backing it and the fact that it was easier for military bands to play than *Vande Mataram*.

The Tribune, 5 August 1995

Vision of India

Our historians have done a devilish job creating stereotypes of different communities. Since Muslims ruled over the country for several centuries they distorted their image to suit their themes. Deep inside the non-Muslim psyche was embedded the conviction that most Muslim rulers were bigots and vandals who smashed idols, destroyed temples, slaughtered infidels as well as cows. A few exceptions like Akbar and Zainul Abedin are highlighted as exceptions to the rule. Now read this testament written by a Muslim monarch to his son and heir to guess the name of its author:

'Oh son! The kingdom of India is full of different religions. Praised be God that He bestowed upon thee its sovereignty. It is incumbent on thee to wipe all religious prejudices off the tablet of thy heart, administer justice according to the way of every religion. Avoid especially the sacrifice of the cow by which thou canst capture the hearts of the people of

India and subjects of this country may be found up with royal obligations.

'Do not ruin the temple and shrines of any community which is obeying the law of government. Administer justice in such a manner that the King be pleased with the subjects and the subjects with the King. The cause of Islam can be promoted more by the sword of obligation than by the sword of tyranny.'

It was written by Babar to his son Humayun.

Sunday, 27 April 1985

■

Indo-Pak *bhai-bhaism*

Right from the time of the partition of the sub-continent in 1947 I have been of the view that friendship with Pakistan should be India's top priority in its dealings with foreign nations. I was for giving Pakistan whatever it needed: wheat, rice, coal, steel, cement, even small arms, on preferential terms so that it did not look to other countries for them. In short, make Pakistan into a friendly neighbour dependent on India. I would have unilaterally abolished the need for visas for Pakistanis visiting India and shamed them into doing the same for Indians visiting Pakistan. Such a policy would not only have made Pakistan incapable of waging war against us but also given Indian Muslims a sense of security as well as ungrudging loyalty to the country.

Unfortunately, this was not the way our government envisaged Indo-Pak relations. It was never able to get over the distrust generated by the demand for a separate State, and instead of accommodating Pakistan as far as it could, it adopted a policy of confrontation. As a consequence, instead of having a reliant, militarily weak and friendly neighbour, we have one who prefers to pay more to other nations for what it could get cheaper from us; militarily strong, and hostile towards us. Our foreign policy towards Pakistan has been a dismal failure because it lacked the compassion which an elder and much stronger brother should have towards the younger. Our media has, by and large, toed the official line by periodically spreading canards of Pakistani designs to attack India and accusing it of fomenting insurgency in Kashmir and Punjab.

I for one looked forward to the visit of Benazir Bhutto's personal envoy, Abdul Sattar, to India. She could not have chosen a better emissary as he had known our prime minister and foreign minister during his tenure as Ambassador in India. Benazir has never met either of them. His mission was limited to renewing personal contacts and seeing whether the two countries could now be steered towards a friendlier course. If we had shown more accommodation on items of minor importance like Siachen and the proposed Woolar Dam, we might have got more cooperation in preventing gun-running and the coming and going of terrorists across Kashmir and Punjab borders.

The Hindustan Times, 20 January 1990

Telephonic exchange of abuses

Every once a week or so, a fellow rings me up to give me a piece of his mind. As soon as he recognizes my 'hello' he begins, '*Abey O! Ulloo kee dum* . . . You, tail of an owl!' Since I know what is going to follow, I interrupt him with the choicest epithets—my range of abusive, insulting vocabulary would bring a blush of shame on the most loud-mouthed harlot plying her trade in Sonagachi or Kamatipura. We have a no-holds-barred slanging match for a good five minutes. When he first started on this exercise, I used to get upset. I thought of reporting him to the telephone authorities to watch his line, report him to the police and have him locked up. It no longer bothers me; on the contrary I look forward to his call. It helps me to refresh my insult vocabulary. One never knows when it may come in handy against a real person rather than an unknown coward who refuses to divulge his entity.

I cannot pretend that I find the exchange of abuse distasteful. I quite enjoy hearing men going for each other—women slangers can be even more fun. Most of the time these squabbles take place between strangers who happen to tread on each other's toes. Hence imputing illegitimacy or sexual intimacy within forbidden degrees of relationships is not taken literally and run like dirty water off a duck's back. It is when a verbal shaft is aimed at a particular individual that it becomes really hurtful. And if the one at the receiving end is not in a position to hit back, it also becomes unfair. It is hitting below the belt. It is not cricket as played by gentlemen. Rajiv Gandhi's reference to Ram Jethmalani as a barking dog was an example of an ungentlemanly jab in the solar plexus. He chose the wrong victim because Jethmalani gave him more in return than he had bargained for.

Coming back to my weekly caller. Since he does not know that I am often out of Delhi, it takes him some time to discover when I have returned. I can catch the tone of surprise in his voice when he asks '*Array, aa gaya? Ulloo kee dum*!' He does not vary his introductory remarks. I tell him that '*Ulloo ka pattha*—son of an owl' is the commoner form than *ullu kee dum,* but perhaps he avoids using it as it applies to him. That really rouses his ire. But the angrier he gets, the more incoherent he becomes. He is also often drunk. When I tell him so, he explodes '*Terey baap ka peeta hoon*? Is it your father's liquor I drink?' No, I assure him that my father does not supply him the liquor and ask him if he knows who his father is. That takes quite some time to sink in. When it does, he explodes again and questions my legitimacy. The last time he rang up and had run through his limited repertoire of abuse, I asked him gently whether or not he had a wife to control his drinking and intemperate language. 'I am not a bloody fool like you,' he replied. 'I am a bachelor and mean to remain one.' That gave me the opening I was waiting for. 'Now I understand,' I said, 'you are a

bachelor, the same as your father was.' And I slammed
down the receiver.

Sunday, 14 November 1987

■

The bathing pool

Come spring and my thoughts turn to swimming pools.
By April it is warm enough to venture into an open-air
pool heated by the sun. In May and June I choose the
cooler waters of one that is covered. And, in both, I
avoid hours when little boys and girls come in droves
armed with nylon wings, snorkels, flippers and rubber
balls and make a bloody nuisance of themselves. I also
avoid early evenings, when paunchy civil servants on
their way home from the secretariat stop by to cool off
and exchange office gossip standing waist deep in the
water. Their sweat is more odiferous than their talk.

I have been a swimming buff all my life. I have
swum in all the world's oceans, many of its seas and
in bathing pools across the globe from New York and
London to Yokohama; from Stockholm, Ankara,
Kampala and down to the underworld in Auckland. I
have quite a repertoire of swimming pool anecdotes
and incidents collected from different countries.

It started off in Lahore where I was in college. I was
among the few who swam all round the year braving
the icy water in the winter months. An episode which

stays in my mind is about a wrestler and a very hairy Sardarji. Both were avid swimmers. The Sardarji was in the habit of using anyone's soap at the shower without ever asking its owner. One day, the wrestler, a Muslim, brought a hair-removing (*baal uraney vaala*) cake of soap. As was his habit, the Sardarji lathered himself lavishly and rubbed the suds into his beard and hairy torso. The wrestler made a quick getaway. When the results of the operation came off in clumps in his hands, the Sardarji's ire knew no bounds. He did the rounds of all the hostels with a *kirpan* in his hand and swore he would kill the wrestler. The wrestler discreetly asked for permission to migrate. He left Government College and joined Islamia where he felt safer.

The first thing I did when I arrived in England to study for the Bar was to join the YMCA which had a heated swimming pool. It was after I had paid my subscription and gone for my first swim that I was sternly told by the instructor that no kind of swimming suits or bathing trunks were allowed in the pool: you had to be stark naked. This was apparently a precaution against people with venereal disease using the pool. Like all Indians, I was too embarrassed to expose myself. My subscription went to waste. Thereafter, most of my swimming was done during summer months in the lakes and rivers of England.

It was at Izmir (Turkey) that I had the most memorable bathing pool experience. The hotel had an elevated pool with walls made of plate glass through which you could see the swimmers in the water. A young couple were having a lot of fun chasing each other round the pool, diving in and out. Then the girl went up on the diving board. Her boyfriend followed her and threatened to push her off. She hesitated a while before poising for a dive. The boy grabbed the top half of her bikini just as she leapt off the board. The bikini snapped and the girl plunged in topless. A sight for the Gods! The poor girl came out with her arms covering her shapely bosom and a torrent of abuse in Turkish for her boyfriend, who was sheepishly holding a towel for her to cover her nakedness.

Water has a strange fascination for some people. Bernard Shaw was one of them. He wrote of an incident when some boys took a bet over giving the bearded patriarch a ducking. One of them accepted the wager and swam stealthily towards the playwright who was swimming at the other end of the pool. As the boy approached from behind, Shaw suddenly turned round to face him. The boy was overcome with embarrassment. Shaw asked him what he was up to. The boy told him about the bet. 'That's all right,' said Shaw, 'let me take a deep breath, then you can give me a ducking and win your bet.'

Byron and Shelley could also never resist water. While Byron was a powerful swimmer, Shelley never learnt to swim. They often went out boating together. More than once their boat overturned and Byron had to rescue Shelley. When Shelley died, it was from drowning.

Swimming is rated much the best of all exercises; it

exercises every muscle of the body evenly without overstraining the arms or legs as happens in games like tennis, badminton, hockey, soccer or jogging. The one disadvantage it has is that it exposes you to any diseases that the other people in the pool might suffer from. You really have to relax your views on hygiene when you enter a club or a hotel swimming pool. Water flows in and out of swimmers' mouths, nostrils and other orifices to pass into yours. It can be worse when there are little children in the same pool. It is this that gave currency to the oft-quoted joke: 'Spell psychology' someone asks you. You spell it. He comes out with the punch line—'Correct! P silent as in swimming.'

Sunday, 8 July 1989

■

The task of seeing oneself

The gods in their wisdom did not grant me the gift of seeing myself as others see me. They must have thought knowing what others thought of me might engender suicidal tendencies in me and decided to let me stew in my own self-esteem. Now I am up against the formidable task of having to write about myself. It is a daunting assignment.

Have you ever tried to look at yourself squarely in the eyes in your own mirror? Try it and you will understand what I mean. Within a second or two you

will turn your gaze from your eyes to other features—
as women do when they are putting on make-up or
men do when they are shaving. Looking into the depths
of one's own eyes reveals the naked truth. The naked
truth about oneself can be very ugly.

I know I am an ugly man. Physical ugliness has
never bothered me nor inhibited me from making
overtures to the fairest of women. I am convinced that
only empty-headed nymphomaniacs look out for
handsome gigolos. They have no use for the likes of
me; I have no use for the likes of them. My concern is
not with my outward appearance, my untidy turban,
unkempt beard or my glazed look (I have been told
that my eyes are that of a lustful *badmaash*) but what
lies behind the physical—the real me compounded of
conflicting emotions like love and hate, general
irritability and occasional equipoise, angry
denunciation and tolerance of another's point of view,
rigid adherence to self-prescribed regimen and
accommodation of others' convenience. And so on. It
is on these qualities that I will dwell in making an
estimate of myself.

First, I must dispose of the question which people
often ask me: 'What do you think of yourself as a
writer?' Without appearing to wear the false cloak of
humility, let me say quite honestly that I do not rate
myself very highly. I can tell good writing from the
not so good, the first-rate from the passable. I know
that of the Indians or the Indian-born, Nirad
Chaudhuri, Naipaul, Salman Rushdie, Amitava Ghosh

and Vikram Seth handle the English language better than I. I also know I can, and have, written as well as any of the others—R.K. Narayan, Mulk Raj Anand, Mulgaonkar, Ruth Jhabvala, Nayantara Sehgal or Anita Desai. What is more, unlike most in the first or the second category, I have never laid claims to being a great writer. I regard self-praise to be the utmost form of vulgarity. Almost every Indian writer I have met is prone to laud his or her achievement. This is something I have never done. Nor have I ever solicited awards or recognition. Nor ever spread false stories of being considered for the Nobel Prize for literature. The list of prominent Indians who spread such canards about themselves is formidable: Vatsayan (Ageya), G.V. Desani, Dr Gopal Singh Dardi (Governor of Goa), Kamala Das and many others.

Am I a likeable man? I am not sure. I do not have many friends because I do not set much store by friendship. I found that friends, however nice and friendly they may be, demand more time than I am willing to spare. I get easily bored with people and would rather read a book or listen to music than converse with anyone for too long. I have had a few very close friends in my time. I am ashamed to admit that when some of them dropped me, instead of being upset, I felt relieved. And when some died, I cherished their memory more than I did their company when they were alive.

I have the same attitude towards women whom I have liked or loved. It does not take much for me to get deeply emotional about women. Often at the very first meeting I feel I have found the Helen I was seeking, and like Majnoon sifting the sands of desert wastes, my quest for Laila is over. None of these infatuations lasts very long. At times, betrayal of trust hurts me deeply, but nothing leaves lasting scars on my psyche. The only lesson I have learnt is that as soon as you sense the others cooling off, be the one to drop them. Dropping people gives you a sense of triumph; being dropped, one of defeat which leaves the ego wounded.

I do not have the gift of friendship. Nor the gift of loving or being loved. Hate is my stronger passion. Mercifully it has never been directed against a community but only against certain individuals. I hate with a passion unworthy of anyone who would like to describe himself as civilized. I try my best to ignore them but they are like an aching tooth which I am periodically compelled to feel with my tongue to assure myself that it still hurts. My hate goes beyond the people I hate. I even drop those who befriend them. My enemy's friends become my enemies.

Hate does not always kill the man who hates, as is maintained by the sanctimonious. Unrepressed hate can often be a catharsis. Shakespeare could gnash his teeth with righteous hatred:

> You common cry of curs whose breath I hate
> As reek o' the rotten fens, whose loves I prize
> As the dead carcases of unburied men
> That do corrupt the air.

Fortunately, there are not many people I hate. I could count them on the tips of the fingers of one hand—no more than four or five. And if I told you why I hate them, you may agree that they deserve contempt and hatred.

I hate name-droppers. I hate self-praisers. I hate arrogant men. I hate liars. Is there anything wrong in hating them? People ask me, why can't you leave them alone? Why can't you ignore their existence? Now, that is something I cannot do. I cannot resist making fun of name-droppers, calling liars liars to their faces. And I love abusing the arrogant. I have been in trouble many times because of my inability to resist mocking these types. And since most name-droppers, self-praisers and arrogant men go from success to success, become ministers, Governors and win awards they don't deserve, my anger often explodes into denouncing them in print. I have been dragged into courts and before the Press Council. This can be a terrible waste of time and money. I think I will have wax images of my pet hates and vent my spleen on them by sticking pins in their effigies. May the fleas of a thousand camels infest their armpits!

Sunday, 27 June 1987

To each his own grief

There are two schools of thought on the subject of death—eastern and western. Orientals believe that the best way of coping with the death of a loved one like a parent, spouse or child is to cry your heart out till you are drained of tears. The custom, *vaine* (chants of lament), and breast-beating were regarded as cathartic. All this is followed by *chautha, chaaleesveen, bhog, antim-ardas* or a prayer meeting in memory of the departed soul. Friends are expected to call, in the belief that grief shared is grief halved. Westerners believe that grief is a private matter and should not be exhibited in public. Shedding tears is unmanly. One should put up a stoic front and get over the loss by oneself.

I had to cope with the problem myself very recently. Being an agnostic, I could not find solace in religious ritual. Being essentially a loner, I discouraged friends and relations coming to condole with me on the death of my wife. Most of them ignored my request. I found this commiserating with me an emotional trauma. I spent the first night alone sitting in my chair in the dark. At times I broke down. But soon recovered my composure. A couple of days later, I resumed my usual routine of work from dawn to dusk. That took my mind off the stark reality of having to live alone in an empty home for the rest of my days. But friends persisted on calling. And upsetting my equilibrium. So I packed myself off to Goa to be by myself. I am not sure if it will work out.

Everyone has to evolve his or her own formula for coping with grief. People who believe in god turn to him. The words of the 34th Psalm are pertinent: 'The Lord is close to the broken-hearted and saves those who are crushed in spirit.' Jesus Christ was not ashamed of weeping before everyone when he lost a friend: 'When Jesus saw Many weeping and the Jews who had come along with him also weeping, he was deeply marred in spirit and troubled: "Where have you laid him?" he asked. "Come and see Lord," they replied. Jesus wept. Then the Jews said, "See how he loved him!"' (John 11:33:38)

As one would expect, Osho Rajneesh made light of the darkest of subjects including ways of coping with grief. In his collection of sermons, *Walking in Zen, Sitting in Zen*, he cites the case of an Italian, Perelli, and his unusual method of getting over the shock of losing his wife: 'At the funeral of his wife, Perelli made a terrible scene, so terrible and heart-rending, in fact, that friends had to forcibly restrain him from jumping into the grave and being buried with his beloved, Maria. Then, still overcome with grief, he was taken home in the rented limousine and immediately went into complete seclusion.

'A week passed and nothing was heard of him. Finally, worried about the poor guy, his late wife's brother went to the house. After ringing the doorbell for ten minutes—and still worried—the brother-in-law jimmied the front door, went upstairs and found his dead sister's husband busily banging the maid.

'The bedroom was a mess—empty champagne bottles everywhere.

'"This is terrible, Perelli!" the brother-in-law declared in shocked tones. "Your dead wife, my sister, has been dead only a week and you're doing this! You're doing this!"

'So busy in the saddle was Perelli, that he managed only to turn his head. "How do I know what I'm doing?" he said, "I got such grief! I got such grief!"'

The Telegraph, 26 January 2002